TAMING THE FRENCH TYCOON

TAMING THE FRENCH TYCOON

BY

REBECCA WINTERS

First published in Great Britain 2015
by Mills & Boon, an imprint of Harlequin (UK) Limited,
Large Print edition 2015
Eton House, 18-24 Paradise Road,
Richmond, Surrey, TW9 1SR

ISBN: 978-0-263-25633-8

Harlequin (UK) Limited's policy is to use papers that are natural, renewable and recyclable products and made from wood grown in sustainable forests. The logging and manufacturing processes conform to the legal environmental regulations of the country of origin.

Printed and bound in Great Britain
by CPI Antony Rowe, Chippenham, Wiltshire

CHAPTER ONE

May

WITH HIS BANKING business done in Cyprus, Luc had taken a rare morning off to visit Yeronisos before flying back to France. He'd always had an interest in archaeology and the tiny island off the coast was thought to be the site of the temple of Apollo. They'd dug up foundations, walls, coins, amulets, wine jugs, and much more. So far the items had been traced to Alexandria, three hundred miles away.

Evidently Cleopatra, queen of Egypt, had possessed the resources to build here on the top of these seventy-foot cliffs that kept visitors away. Yeronisos was so inaccessible they called it a virgin island because it had remained much as it had been when man had first come there over ten thousand years ago.

Luc had walked around the excavations for an hour and found it a totally fascinating place where he could indulge his passion, but then a boatload of male teenagers had arrived in a dinghy to disturb its tranquility. Instead of studying antiquities, they'd come to cliff dive, a foolhardy pursuit with the waters churning at the base because of a swift current. There was a sign that forbade it, but this group paid no heed.

Deciding it was time to go, he descended the steep steps. The warm May sun forced him to put on his sunglasses to cut the glint reflecting off the deep blue water. When he looked out, another dinghy was approaching. He returned to the speedboat he'd rented and started untying the ropes at the dock.

While he was doing so, the boat pulled in behind him and more young divers jumped out. He recognized their eagerness as they scrambled up the side of the island to get to the top and challenge the elements.

Stepping into his boat, he happened to glance at the last guy to leave the dinghy. But it turned out to be a young woman wearing a backpack. She had a pair of the most fabulous long legs he'd ever seen. A T-shirt over her bikini couldn't hide the voluptuous mold of her body. A dark braid circled her well-shaped head.

As she passed him, he found himself staring into an incredibly lovely face. Classic, with high cheekbones and a provocative mouth. She reminded him a little of Sabine, the girl he'd loved and lost in a plane crash years ago, but sunglasses covered this woman's eyes so he couldn't see their color. With her attention focused on the top of the cliff, he doubted she'd noticed him. She'd come here with all those hormone-filled idiots?

In the background came the excited shouts from the divers already launching themselves into the dangerous, swirling waters. One by one, they jumped into the huge swells and then had to swim for their lives to reach the rocky walls of the cliff. When he heard several blood-curdling screams among the shouts, his emotions suddenly morphed into gut-wrenching pain as he was transported back to his last year in high school.

During those years he and his friends had felt immortal. In their crazy exuberance, they'd decided to go skydiving. But it had ended in horror when their plane crashed against a hillside. Out of the six, four of them survived. The other two had perished, one of them being Sabine.

His fear for the divers' safety intensified, causing his body to tense. Any one of them could be killed doing something so reckless. Luc knew all about it. He broke out in a cold sweat watching the attractive female make her way to the bottom of the steps that would take her to the top of the cliff. He thought of Sabine and couldn't bear to see this woman hurt or possibly killed doing something so reckless.

She was young like they'd once been, eager for adventure and heedless of the danger. Didn't she know her body could be tossed against the rocks and knocked unconscious or worse? Fearful for the welfare of this beautiful woman, he climbed out onto the dock again and called to her.

She stopped and turned around. "Yes?" she answered in French. "Were you speaking to me?"

The sight of her made his heart beat faster, a reaction he hadn't felt for a woman in years. "Haven't you read the sign? No cliff jumping! You heard those screams. Don't you realize that what your group is doing could end in fatalities?"

Her arched brows frowned. "If it's your job to enforce the rule, you should have stopped the group in the first dinghy."

He moved closer to her. "It's anyone's job to stop a bunch of headstrong young people from bringing harm to themselves." Without thinking he said, "I'd hate to see a lovely woman like you lose your life for a thrill. Have you no concern for your family or loved ones who would be devastated if anything happened to you?" Luc would never forget the pain.

She stared at him for a full minute. One corner of her mouth lifted in a mocking curve. *"Félicitations, monsieur.* That's the most original pick-up line any Frenchman has ever thrown at me and believe me, I've heard the best of them."

Frenchman? That was an odd thing for her to say since *she* was French. Her response stunned him in more ways than one. "You think that's what I'm doing?"

"It looks that way to me. I'm wondering how often you loiter at the dock, lying in wait for an unsuspecting, accessible female to detain."

"What?" he almost hissed the word.

"If I'm wrong...*je regrette.*" She shrugged her shoulders. "Is it possible you never did anything so daring as cliff jump when you were young? Might I point out that you took your life in your hands just coming out here in your speedboat rental?"

Luc had to tamp down his temper, caught between his concern for her welfare and her provocative insinuations about him. "In what way?" his voice grated.

"Surely you know the Mediterranean has its share of great white sharks. What are you? Approaching forty? I hope you're still a good swimmer in case you should meet with an accident at sea. A rental boat isn't always reliable, but try to enjoy your sedentary day anyway instead of attempting to ruin it for everyone else. *Ciao.*"

In the next breath, she started up the steps with surprising speed to reach her destination.

Between the disturbing flashback and their shocking conversation, Luc had been thrown into a particularly foul mood. He got in the boat without looking back. Once he'd started the engine and edged away from the dock, he headed for the mainland.

When he thought about it, he could imagine that many a man had lain in wait for her, thus her ready defense, which was damn off-putting. The female who'd clashed with him was probably twenty, maybe twenty-one, but he'd found out she could take care of herself without effort. Before the plane crash he might have done exactly what she'd accused him of doing in order to get to know her.

To his chagrin, the vision of the captivating young woman stayed with him long after his flight home, as he picked up his car at the airport and drove to his villa in Cagnes-sur-Mer outside Nice. In that moment when he could imagine their outing ending in tragedy, the memory of the plane crash had swept over him. He'd wanted to spare her from plunging to her death. Instead she'd managed to get under his skin.

Though born with an adventurous spirit, he was no longer willing to take risks when life was so precious. Over the last fifteen years he'd grown particularly cautious when it came to making landmark business decisions that could affect not only his professional life, but his family's welfare and reputation.

The plane crash had changed him into a different person. He'd learned the meaning of mortality. That caution had also kept him out of involved personal relationships that could put his emotions in jeopardy. It was the reason he hadn't cut the motor and reached for his binoculars to watch her defy danger because she thought she was immortal. He needed to put her and the incident out of his mind.

Jasmine reached the top of the island with only a little time to spare. The dinghy full of guys eager to cliff dive had been rented for two hours. Since this group of teens had room in the boat for her, she'd ridden to the island with them, glad she didn't have to drive a boat herself.

While they jumped, this would be her one and only chance to take pictures of the excavations before she couriered the negatives to the publisher. With this last task done, the book could be printed by the end of the month and ready for the distribution date. She was no photographer, but it didn't matter as long as they turned out.

To her chagrin, the encounter with the man at the dock had shaken her. He wasn't anything like André, the French guy with the seductive way of talking. She'd dated him a little at university before dropping him because he'd turned out to be way too controlling. But just now, when the stranger in sunglasses had come at her about the dangers of cliff jumping, she had been reminded of André, and her adrenaline had taken over in a negative way.

With hindsight, Jasmine realized she'd been ruder to this man than any male she'd ever met. The trouble was, with his unruly black hair and strong masculine features, he was *all* male and breathtaking in those white shorts that hung low on his hips.

Her instant attraction to him had come as a tremendous surprise. That was why his erroneous conclusion about her reason for being there had caused her temper to flare. She wasn't some foolish teenager, yet he'd put her in that category. Little did he know, she thought the cliff jumpers were crazy too, but she'd grown up with older brothers and knew you couldn't stop them if they saw a challenge.

If only the man had just stopped there, but he hadn't. It was the mention of family that had hit a nerve where her guilt lurked. Where did he get off implying that Jasmine didn't care about them? The intensity of his attack had caught her on the raw, creating a negative reaction in her that went volatile.

In retaliation, she'd hurtled little insults back at him like darts thrown at balloons, hoping to damage his ego, but she doubted he'd felt them. He was most likely in his early thirties. Being rock-hard lean and fit, she imagined he could outswim a shark. Deep down, she knew he was the kind of man who could have any woman he wanted and didn't need to hang around some lonely outpost waiting for an opportunity.

For the next hour, she concentrated on her task, trying to shake off the encounter. Once finished, she went back down to the dock and ate her lunch while she waited in the dinghy for the others. The speedboat had long since gone. She wondered what the man had been doing there in the first place, but why she cared was quite beyond her when she was still smarting from their confrontation.

Pretty soon, the first dinghy filled up and took off. A few minutes later, the others divers came running. She learned that one of the guys had cut his lower leg open. Someone had wrapped it in a towel, but he needed medical help. They left for the mainland, where she'd parked her rental car at the boating concession.

Jasmine looked around, but didn't see the man with whom she'd traded insults. She was relieved he hadn't been there to watch them come ashore with the injured teen. She could just imagine his "I told you so" smirk as the guy was lifted into the ambulance.

There was something wrong for her still to be thinking about him. Determined to put the incident behind her, she got in her car and drove the short distance to Nicosia. From the airport there she would catch her afternoon flight back to France.

Later in the day, when the plane began its descent to the Nice airport, it dawned her that the stranger had spoken with a distinct, cultured Niçois accent. A small shiver raced through her body to think he might actually live here, but the chances of bumping into him again were astronomical. How absurd to imagine such a thing happening.

For the second time today, she had to ask herself why it mattered when she had earthshaking events on her mind and little time to accomplish all that had to be done by midsummer.

July

When the phone rang at six-thirty a.m. Friday morning, Jasmine was awake, but she hadn't gotten out of bed yet. To her shock, she'd been dreaming about the stranger on Yeronisos again. Visions of him had been filtering through her mind for the last two months and she was sick of it. Her fantasy of seeing him again was absolutely crazy!

Thank heaven today was her twenty-sixth birthday, the day she and her papa had planned out in detail before his death. She could put aside the memory of this man who'd been haunting her dreams and deal with real problems. Jasmine glanced at the caller ID. Sure enough it was Robert Lambert, her grandfather's attorney, calling right on cue.

Jasmine clicked on. *"Bonjour,* Robert."

"Bon anniversaire to you, Jasmine. I know it's early, but we don't have a lot of time before the staff meeting at ten in the conference room."

"I'll be ready." She'd been getting ready for this day for a long, long time.

"Excellent. Per your grandfather's wishes, you will be interviewed in his laboratory for tonight's six o'clock news. The arrangements have already been made. He wanted it announced over the air before the day was out to quiet anyone who wasn't on board."

"I'm all prepared for it."

Not only had her grandfather hated publicity, he'd never let outsiders step foot inside his laboratory. For him to sanction a television interview in the place where he'd worked all his life indicated an intimacy between him and Jasmine the viewers couldn't possibly misinterpret.

"Meet me at nine-thirty to discuss one more

matter with you before everyone else arrives at ten. Do you have any questions?"

"No. At this point I want to thank you for all you've done and are doing to help me. I couldn't do this without you. Papa knew that."

"We both miss your papa. Knowing where he is now, I'm sure he's happy this day has come for many reasons."

"I agree. See you soon."

They both clicked off.

It was really happening.

The second she hung up, her phone rang again. She glanced at the caller ID. This time it was her parents. Recurring guilt stabbed at her because she was spending yet another birthday away from home. Thankfully it would be for the last time.

After picking up, she cried, "Mom? Dad?"

"It's your dad, my darlin' birthday girl. We miss you so much, we gathered the whole family together and decided to fly over to celebrate this weekend with you."

A soft gasp escaped. "You mean you're *here*?"

"Yes. All twelve of us. We just landed. Your mom's helping Melissa with Cory, or she'd get on the phone. Your three-year-old nephew has a hard time sitting still. We'll be at the house in an hour."

Jasmine could hardly take it in. They had no idea about the elaborate plans she and her papa had made. They didn't know that today she would be attending a board meeting that was going to change history.

Instead of phoning them after it was over as she'd intended, she would have to divulge the secret she and her grandfather had been planning the minute they arrived at the house. In truth, she was thrilled they'd come. She'd never needed their support more. "I—I can't wait to see you," she said in a tremulous voice.

"You don't know the half of it, Sparkles. See you in a little while."

"Oh, Dad—" Emotions of love and guilt made her throat swell before she heard the click. He'd called her that from the time she was a little girl.

What made this so hard was the fact that she hadn't always been home for important events.

Since her grandparents had died, she'd been working secretly behind the scenes to develop a perfume to help save the company. Her papa had sworn her to secrecy, even from her parents.

For the last few months, she'd felt estranged from them, which had never happened before. Her dad was particularly upset for her mother, who was missing Jasmine terribly and didn't understand why she hadn't been home for so long. When they'd hung up, Jasmine had felt his crushing disappointment and it had almost destroyed her.

But now that it was her birthday, everything was going to change. Within a month she would set certain things right and then go home to her family and spend the rest of her life proving her love for them. Her silly idea of marrying a cowboy was a fantasy of course, but she *was* going home for good!

After hanging up, she alerted the housekeeper that her family would be descending within the hour. Then she hurried to shower and wash her hair. To her shock, the stranger's comment about her lack of concern for her family's feelings unexpectedly flashed through her mind again, pressing on her awful guilt..

It infuriated her that the memory of his off-base remarks lingered to torment her. She couldn't believe that after two months she was still thinking about him when she had a board meeting to dress for. Jasmine had never attended one, but knew she needed to wear something conservative.

Her new three-piece suit with the knit jacket, pencil skirt and shell in soft peach would project the right image. Not over-or underdressed. She'd wear her hair caught back at the nape and put on her small pearl earrings. This was the kind of outfit her grandmother would have worn to such a meeting with Jasmine's papa.

Luc realized he needed a break from banking business and was ready for a relaxing weekend. But when he called his good friend Nic Valfort to go deep-sea fishing, he learned Nic was on a trip to the States with his new wife and wouldn't be back for another three days.

Somehow Luc needed to throw off this obsession over the woman on Yeronisos. Why in the hell couldn't he get her out of his mind? He'd found himself fantasizing about her, which was ridiculous when he knew he'd never see her again.

Somehow he had to think about something else. Being with Nic would have helped. He and Nic had met at college and had been friends ever since, like their grandfathers, who'd done business together in the past.

Between the plane crash that had marred Luc's life and the tragedy that had befallen Nic's first wife, the men had suffered grief at different periods and could relate. Luc enjoyed being with him whenever they could break away.

But since Nic's second marriage, they hadn't seen much of each other. His friend was ecstatically happy with his new American wife.

After he got back from California, Luc would call him so they could get together.

As for tonight, there would be a party with his family to celebrate one of his cousin's birthdays. While he was getting ready to leave his suite, his assistant, Thomas, buzzed him. It had better be important because he was already late.

"Oui?"

"I just got a heads-up from one of our sources in Paris. Turn on your TV. Hurry!"

"More terrorism?"

"This news could be worse for us depending on the outcome."

A frown marred Luc's Gallic features. He reached for the remote in his desk drawer and clicked on to the six o'clock news. He paid Thomas well to keep his ear to the ground.

"Good evening, everyone. On this Friday, we're coming to you from Chaine Huit in Paris, France, with breaking news that is already rocking the international perfuming community. Today, a stunning announcement came from Grasse, France, the perfume capital of the world, causing a negative fluctuation in the stock market."

Tension lines deepened around Luc's mouth.

"Within the last twenty-four hours, the iconic House of Ferrier has undergone a dramatic new change in management."

A cold sweat broke out on his body. *What change?* No one had informed Luc.

The former biggest moneymaker in the perfume industry was one of the bank's top clients and had been for ninety years. But two years ago the head of Ferriers had died and the business had slowly started losing revenue. A few months later, Luc's own grandfather had passed away of a bad heart, making Luc the CEO of the bank.

Though the world didn't know it yet, the quarterly gross sales reports indicated a declining percentage in Ferriers's profits. Not totally alarming yet, but still, Luc was worried. Since his grandfather had been Maxim Ferrier's banker, Luc had been the one to take over their various accounts in order to maximize the assets in an unstable economy. It was one of the reasons he'd gone to Nicosia in May and again in June.

But without the proper leadership he'd worried about the future of a company that had been part of the backbone of the French economy for close to a century. If it failed, the economic structure of Southern France would be jeopardized. Like many other businesses, Ferriers had stayed alive all these years. If it continued to go downhill, the bank would be affected.

"Two years ago, the world lost the greatest perfumer of our time, Maxim Ferrier, at sixty-eight years of age. Balmain, Dior, Givenchy, Caron, Guerlain, Chanel, Balenciaga, Estee Lauder, Rochas, Fragonard, Ricci, Lentheric— all the great major perfume houses considered him an icon the world will never see again.

"Since his death, the company has been run by the family and other staff who made up the board while he was alive. But today, they have finally appointed a new head."

Luc ground his teeth. As he'd already found

out, none of them had the Midas touch of the legendary perfumer himself. Who in heaven's name would they have found and brought in to turn things around? Absolutely no one from any other perfume house in the world had Maxim Ferrier's genius. Not in this generation. Probably not for another hundred years.

"Spill it!" Luc muttered furiously to the TV anchorman, who knew this broadcast was making the kind of news the media lived and died for and was milking it for all he was worth.

"Our station is the first to announce the name of Jasmine Martin, a total unknown, who has been put at the helm. She's an unmarried twenty-six-year-old with no formal job experience and has brought no resume to the position of the multibillion-dollar corporation."

"What?" In a state of shock, Luc shot to his feet.

"It's an unprecedented move since only two men have ever held that coveted position in the Ferrier perfume empire...Maxim Ferrier, and before him, his uncle, Paul Ferrier, whose father had run a flower farm in the very beginning. Right now, we're taking you live to the sacrosanct laboratory of the brilliant perfumer in Grasse. Our anchorman, Michel Didier, is standing by there, ready to interview her."

While Luc walked over to the TV screen to get a closer look, the other anchorman introduced himself.

"Good evening from our network in Grasse. I've been invited inside the room where Maxim Ferrier himself developed his famous formula for Night Scent, a perfume that won every award and still tops perfume sales around the globe. This is a privilege for me and all our viewers. The whole world is waiting to meet you, Jasmine. May I call you that?"

"Of course."

As the camera panned in on her, a cry of shock escaped Luc's throat. *No—it couldn't be!*

Hers was the beautiful face he'd seen at the dock on Yeronisos! He took a deep breath, trying to comprehend it. The woman who'd given Luc battle before he'd watched her charge up those steep steps, possibly to her death, was *Jasmine Martin? The new CEO at Ferriers?*

His dark head reared. He'd never thought to see her again. Yet there she was in the flesh, that fiery beauty he'd been fantasizing about every night.

How was it that she of all people on this planet had been made head of one of the most iconic companies in France? She was a daredevil who'd insinuated that Luc was on his way to middle age before she'd ignored him and gone straight up the cliff to jump off. He rubbed the back of his neck in consternation.

It defied logic that a woman so careless with her own life was now running a billion-dollar corporation. Luc was so incredulous over what had been announced, he couldn't make sense of anything.

This evening she wore her hair caught back at the nape. Instead of wearing a T-shirt and bikini, she was dressed in a peach-colored suit that revealed her gorgeous figure.

Behind her were stacked rows of hundreds

of bottles, reminding him of the wizard's shop in the Harry Potter film he'd seen with two of his nephews. Those magic potions that still delighted moviegoers everywhere.

Yet the potions behind this woman had worked their own special magic in the cosmetic world, yielding billions of dollars in revenue.

"I have many questions to ask. But for all those watching our broadcast around the globe, this question is foremost in everyone's mind. How did *you* of all people, of all women, get picked, and at such a young age?"

An impish smile broke out on her alluring face. Luc's breath caught. The memory of their heated exchange had caused him one restless night after another since his return. Twenty-six meant she was older than he'd thought, but it still rankled that she'd dared to accuse him of trying to pick her up.

She folded her arms and lounged against the edge of the lab table.

"You're going to get your scoop now, Michel," she teased with that same audacious maturity, so at odds with her lack of judgment when it came to her safety. There was a twinkle in her dark blue eyes. The first time they'd met she'd been wearing sunglasses. Luc had to admit he'd never seen anyone so natural in front of the camera. "I'm Maxim Ferrier's youngest grand-child."

Grandchild?

The well-known anchorman was taken by total surprise and looked as blown away as Luc felt.

"Since I came along last of his twenty-one grandchildren, he nicknamed me Jasmine. That's because Jasmine is the flower harvested last in October. He said it was his favorite flower because of its beguiling scent. Though my parents named me Blanchette after my mother, his name for me stuck."

Michel shook his head. "Just keep talking. I won't interrupt because I'm speechless and en-chanted, and I know everyone else is too."

Her gentle laugh reached down to burrow in-side a disbelieving Luc, who couldn't comprehend any of it. "I used to hang around my papa. I thought of him as this amazing sorcerer and pretended to be his apprentice. He never seemed to mind."

"Obviously not," the journalist interjected. "Tell the audience why you think he chose you to run the company."

"He once told me I was the only one in the family who got the nose. Not his own children and not any of his grandchildren got it, he said. Just me. I thought he meant I had a Roman nose like a horse. I was so hurt I ran out of the lab crying. He had no idea how much I loved him, but I was horrified that he thought I was ugly."

The anchorman laughed heartily, but Luc's throat closed up with emotion. Children were so literal, as he'd learned from being around his own nieces and nephews.

"Then he came after me and explained what he meant. He said I was so smart, he thought I knew what a nose was. He said I had a beautiful nose like my grandma. But he was referring to the fact that after sixty years, another perfumer had been born in the family, someone like himself who could identify scents. That person was *moi* and he was overjoyed."

Michel smiled. "No wonder he named you to succeed him."

"I still can't believe he did that and I am still trying to come to grips with it. No one could ever fill his shoes. I'm stunned to think he believed I could."

"I'm not surprised you're in shock," the anchorman commented at last. He stared at the camera. "*Mesdames et messieurs*, you couldn't make up a Cinderella story as unusual as this, not in a hundred years. I wish we had more time for the interview. Before we have to end this segment, the audience wants to hear about your grandmother.

"We know she was a great beauty right up to the time of her passing. Not only was she a devoted wife, she was a great intellect who authored several books."

"She was fabulous."

"While you were growing up, you must have

known over the years that the international press touted them the most beautiful couple in the world. The French have called them the Charles Boyer and Marlene Dietrich of the modern era. American media labeled him more handsome and sophisticated than Cary Grant. She has been compared to Grace Kelly and Princess Diana. What do you say to that, Jasmine?"

"What more can I add? They were beautiful people from that era, inside and out. She loved him so much, she died three months later."

Luc hated to admit it, but part of him was spellbound by her and knew the anchorman was too.

"After seeing this broadcast, people will say you inherited her beauty."

"No woman could ever compare to her. If you could have heard my papa on the subject. If ever a man loved a woman..."

Luc heard the tremor in her voice and couldn't help but be moved by her humility. He could never have imagined this side of her after their explosive meeting on Yeronisos. *Unless this was all playacting.* If so, she was the greatest actress he'd ever known.

"Is it true he never gave an interview in his life?"

"That's right. He disliked publicity of any kind. I'm only doing this one interview because our family has been besieged by the media for years. The outpouring of public sentiment over their deaths has been so touching and over-whelming, I hoped to be able to thank them through your program."

"It's a personal honor for me, Ms. Martin. Would it be too forward of me to ask if there's a special man in your life?"

"Since you asked so nicely, I'll answer with a 'yes, it would.'" But she said it with a mock-ing little curve of her mouth that made Luc's emotions churn in remembrance of her errone-ous assumption about him. The anchorman was quick to recover, but he looked embarrassed. Luc knew what it felt like to be slammed by her like that, although she'd been gentler with the other man.

"Message received. Wasn't your grandfather the one who coined the phrase, 'Provence is God's garden'?"

"Oh, no, but he often expressed that sentiment to me."

"While you've been talking, I found another passage in your grandmother's book where she quotes him. He must have been writing about you.

"'Jasmine seems to be a flower made for nostalgia. It grows in doorways and winds over arches, linking it to the intimacy of home. It begins to bloom as the days become hotter, and it releases its scent at the hour when tables are set in the garden or in narrow lanes. It is associated with the melancholy of dusk and the conviviality of summer evenings. Its fragrance permeates the air, making it a background for love.'"

She cleared her throat. "I remember him saying those words. I think Papa had a love affair with flowers all his life."

Watching this interview had tied Luc in knots.

The woman he'd met two months ago was nothing like the flower just described.

The anchorman nodded. "For those of you who still aren't aware, the book Jasmine's grandmother wrote, *Where There's Smoke*, is the definitive source on the life work of Maxim Ferrier. It's being reissued in a second edition with several sections of new information to coincide with the announcement of the new head of Ferriers and will be out on the stands tomorrow. When the first edition of the book came out, it became number one on bestseller lists worldwide. I confess I was enthralled by it."

"Thank you. Grandma worked on it for years. After my papa died, she had it published to honor him."

"No one knew him better than she did, except for you, who came in a close second." Again Luc saw the secret curve in her smile that reminded him of the way she'd smiled at him before letting him have it. The sensation twisted his gut as much now as then.

"Let me read one last thing your grandmother

quoted from her husband. 'An exceptional perfume has a top note to entice, followed by the
rich character of its middle note. Then comes
the end note to bind all three, supplying the
depth and solidity needed to make a lasting signature.' He was a poet, wasn't he?"

"Papa was so many things, I hardly know
where to begin."

"I wish we didn't have to stop. Thank you for
letting us see inside your world. It's been an
honor and privilege."

"For me too."

"Congratulations on your new position, chosen by the head man himself. What greater
endorsement, *n'est-ce pas*?" He turned to the
camera. "That's it for now from Grasse. Back
to you in Paris."

Luc shut off the TV, stunned out of his mind
by her interview. A bomb had been dropped. He
was still trying to recover from the fallout. Pacing the floor, he realized this meant he would be
dealing with *her* in the future. His heart thudded at the very thought of it.

Now that the news had gone global, anything could happen and probably had behind closed doors at Ferriers. He couldn't imagine the members of the Ferrier board, twice or triple her age and most of them family, tolerating the granddaughter to become the head of the company. If they knew what Luc knew...

This was nepotism at its best. Either Maxim Ferrier had become senile toward the end, or she'd had him wrapped around her little finger because she'd inherited his gift. But that gift didn't mean she had the grasp for business or the necessary ability to run one of the most famous companies in existence. There'd been no mention of her education. She had no work experience. As far as he was concerned, she had no common sense either.

The Ferrier board had to have the same opinion about her and would soon find a way to vote her out. But until then Luc would have to be extra careful how he proceeded when the day came he had his first business meeting with her. Frankly, he couldn't imagine it after their explosive encounter on the island. Yet, to his dismay, the thought of being with her again charged every cell in his body.

"Luc?"

It had been a long time since Thomas had walked in without knocking, but Luc understood why. His assistant looked dazed. "I never saw or heard anything so amazing in my life."

"You're not alone, Thomas."

"She's more beautiful than her grandmother was, if that's possible."

It *was* possible. The image of her standing at the base of the cliff had never left him. But there were imperfect parts of her the camera hadn't seen, parts that he felt spelled a lot more trouble for Ferriers.

"I still can't believe she's the new face and power at Ferriers. She may be Maxim Ferrier's favorite and worth millions herself, but she looks too young and defenseless to go to battle against dynasty builders with three times her age and experience."

Luc would have thought the same thing if he

hadn't been the recipient of her words, which could slice and dice a man to shreds in seconds. His assistant wouldn't see her as a defenseless woman if he'd watched her attack that rocky island on those breathtaking limbs of hers with the strength and agility of a military frogman.

Thomas's eyes gleamed. "This means that from now on you'll be meeting with her instead of Giles LeC—" he started to say, but Luc stopped him right there because he didn't want to hear it. He needed time for the news to sink in first.

"I'm late for a party and have to run. See you on Monday." He left by his private exit. It opened into a hallway leading to the private parking lot with a security guard.

Ever since the incident in Cyprus, he'd fought the temptation to find out who she was. A simple phone call to the boating concession that rented dinghies would have told him what he wanted to know, but somehow he'd managed to stop himself in time.

Dieu merci he hadn't let the desire to meet

her in person and set her straight about a few things outweigh his innate caution. Otherwise, she truly would have had the last laugh knowing the director of the Banque Internationale du Midi *was* a voyeur stalking beautiful young women throughout the Mediterranean while on vacation.

The bank couldn't afford to lose one of the biggest accounts since its inception. No matter how acerbic her words, no matter how shallow he found her for being willing to throw her life away for a thrill, no matter how disappointed he was in Maxim Ferrier's decision to put a young loose cannon like her in charge, Luc could do nothing but stand by to watch a catastrophe in the making. And despise himself for being more attracted to her than ever.

CHAPTER TWO

ON WEDNESDAY MORNING, Jasmine saw her family off at Nice airport. She'd promised them that in a month she'd be on her way back home in Idaho for good. Before they boarded the jet, the pain in her parents' eyes revealed their disbelief that she would keep her promise. That look had stabbed her with fresh grief.

They didn't know that the glimpse of her life she'd described in front of the TV camera on Friday belonged to the past. Her grandparents were gone. Once she'd carried out her papa's last wishes—wishes no one else in the whole world knew about except her and his attorney—there was nothing more to keep her in France. But until she'd carried out this plan and moved back to Idaho, they wouldn't believe she really did want to go home for good.

After assuring them that she would arrive in

time for their thirtieth wedding anniversary party in August, she headed for the Banque Internationale du Midi with a growing pit in her stomach.

"Papa?" she said to the air growing hotter by the minute under a July sun. "I carried off the first part of our plan on TV. Now I hope to pull off this second part, but I'm nervous. In case I get into trouble, I'll need your help or I won't be able to put the third part into motion. Do you hear me?"

Last Friday's media announcement had turned the entire Ferrier clan inside out as she had known it would, as her papa, though dead now, had known it would once Robert had read the will at the board meeting.

She knew positively that several of them, including non-family members of the board, had hoped to be named successor when the will was finally read. Of late they'd made no secret about it.

Jasmine's French mother and American father, along with her siblings, were known as the

American faction of her grandparents' progeny. They didn't want to be involved in company business.

But all the other Ferriers lived in France and existed to promote the company. Some of them were situated in Paris with key positions at the perfumery. The rest had never left the environs of Nice that included Grasse. All of them worked for Ferriers in one capacity or other.

In the beginning, there'd been one small foundry in Grasse. In time, thirty distilleries dotted the Basses-Alpes, and the Alpes-Maritime regions. Her papa had his own small private lab in Grasse and eventually divided his time between the perfumery in Hyeres, and the other one in Paris. Little by little, the company expanded until he'd had the big perfumery built in Grasse.

Naturally everyone in the extended family had a huge vested interest in everything that went on. Jasmine loved them all. They were wonderful people. But when it came to families doing business together in a company with a history and heritage like theirs, emotions ran off the charts. Envy, pride and, in some cases, even greed had crept in.

For them to hear that Jasmine of all people had been named, as Michel Didier had said—a woman, the youngest nobody in the family—it had to be the lowest blow of all time.

Her grandfather had been such a private person, it was in keeping with his character to hide his secret agenda until his one great desire had become a fait accompli. Being that he was without a doubt the kindest, most enlightened, generous man she'd ever known, Jasmine had taken his private confidences to her heart. She knew he was counting on her.

Though her papa realized everyone would be upset and hurt one way or another, he'd had a nobler purpose in mind and was using his willing granddaughter to help right a wrong that had gone on since he'd been a small boy raised at La Tourette, the Ferrier home in Grasse.

The family's adverse reaction over Jasmine having been named was nothing compared to the furor that was coming. Tears filled her eyes. "I won't let you down, Papa."

She drove her Audi into the financial district of Nice. The bank that the House of Ferrier had done business with over the years was housed in a former cream-colored palace of neoclassic design. It lay just ahead surrounded with palm trees and exotic flowers. Everything was riding on this visit. Nothing could be accomplished without the bank's help. It was crucial Jasmine get the CEO on her side.

After pulling around to the public parking area, she reached for the file folder she'd brought with her and entered through the main doors. A security guard nodded to her. "May I help you?"

"I'm here to see Monsieur Lucien Charriere on urgent business."

"Do you have an appointment?"

"No, but I'm hoping he'll have time to fit me in to his busy schedule." Her papa had always dealt with Raimond Charriere, but she'd learned from Giles LeClos, Ferrier's comptroller, that he'd passed away within months of her papa. His grandson Lucien had taken over.

"Without an appointment I'm afraid it would be impossible for him to meet with you. If you'll call the bank and ask to be put through to his office, his secretary will know how to help you."

"I'm sorry, but my reason for seeing him can't wait. If you'll please let him know that Jasmine Martin from Ferriers is here in the foyer, I'll wait as long as I have to."

The name Ferrier had always been the magic word and caused the older man's composure to slip. Without asking for picture ID, he pulled out his phone and spoke in hushed tones to the person who answered. When he hung up, he said, "Someone will be right with you. I didn't realize who you were."

"That's perfectly understandable." In a minute she heard, "Ms. Martin?" Jasmine turned in the direction of the man who'd just spoken her name.

"I'm Thomas, Monsieur Charriere's assistant." His eyes fastened on her with blatant male interest. "If you'll come with me, I'll show you to his office. He's on the phone, but he'll be through with his overseas call shortly."

"Thank you."

They walked on marble floors and down the north hallway to a suite that had been modernized. But nothing could hide the fact that it had once been a royal Italian residence of the House of Savoy before Nice was made an arrondissement of Grasse.

Before they reached the double doors of the inner office, they opened. Silhouetted over the threshold stood a tall, thirtyish male who immediately reminded her of…the bad boy at the dock on Yeronisos!

"You!" The shock of seeing him again, of finding him *here*, of realizing who he was, left her reeling. Her fantasy had come true! How was it possible?

Today he was immaculately turned out in a banker's suit and tie. His black hair, almost unruly, looked like he'd run his hand through it a few times out of frustration or habit.

Already he needed another shave and it was only eleven in the morning. She knew what he looked like underneath his clothes. Rock hard and lean, with a hungry look around his compelling mouth and nose. He had the genes of his Ligurian ancestry, which had given him moody black eyes. She hadn't been able to see their color behind his sunglasses.

A woman wouldn't be a woman if she didn't notice him. Jasmine had noticed him all right, and hadn't been the same since. As she'd discovered on the island, he was a standout in any crowd or alone.

She recalled her grandmother's description of her grandfather the first time they met. *The tall, fit, suntanned man with the penetrating black eyes and hair stood before me. He was so handsome he took my breath away.*

Jasmine could relate, but that pit in her stomach enlarged because this man's glittering gaze traveled over her, making every feminine corpuscle in her body quiver. He was still angry over her insults. She could feel it, but she was angry over his too!

Here she'd been afraid that Raimond Charriere's grandson would be a hard sell, though she'd come prepared to influence him until he couldn't say no to her request. How could she possibly have known that the CEO of the most prominent banking institution in the South of France was the man she'd accused of lying in wait to pick up defenseless young women?

A moan escaped her lips. Jasmine could appeal to other bankers, but because Ferriers had done business with *this* bank since the beginning, she wanted this man's help above all. Otherwise, her plan could be dashed to pieces and all would be lost. She couldn't let that happen! Somehow she had to salvage the situation. But after their caustic exchange on the island, his icy smile told her he'd show no mercy. She knew that much in her bones, and it put her on the defensive. She spoke first.

"I take it from your silence that you didn't expect me to survive my outing on Yeronisos."

His eyes narrowed on her features. "From your long, quiet assessment of me just now, I take it you're equally astonished that despite the sharks, I made it back to the mainland in the rental boat in one piece."

She'd just made things worse. "I should have called for an appointment."

One dark brow lifted. "But as you've already demonstrated, you like to live life on the edge so I'm not surprised you didn't go through normal channels. I hardly recognized you from the television broadcast on Friday evening."

Red-hot heat enveloped her. She'd never blushed in her life, but there was always a first time, as she was finding out. It crept from her toenails to the top of her head, missing nothing in between.

"I can only wonder what to expect next." His deep voice cast the final net to capture her total attention.

This was going from bad to worse. "Do you think we could start over again?"

His hands had gone to his hips in an utterly

male stance. "I'm not sure. If I were to say it's a pleasure to meet you, would you assume that one of my secret sedentary activities is to trap hapless females who have the misfortune of entering this old man's lair?"

He wanted an apology. So did she, but since Jasmine had come to him on a desperate mission, it was up to her to cauterize the wound before it bled out of control.

"I'm sorry for the way I reacted on the island. You were right about the danger. One of the guys cut his leg open and he had to be taken to the hospital in an ambulance after we reached the boating concession."

The dangerous glitter in his eyes started to dissipate. "Fortunately for Ferriers, its new CEO survived to live another day."

This man wanted a full apology.

"I didn't honestly believe you were a predator, but your assumptions, especially the one that I gave no thought to the family that loved me, provoked me to say things that shocked even me." Which was the truth.

His black eyes studied her as if he were trying to weigh her sincerity. "I concede that in my concern for your safety, I was a little harsh in my assessment."

A little?

When he extended his hand, she had no choice but to shake it. Of course she was thankful for this overture on his part. *You need him on your side, Jasmine.* But the second she felt skin against skin, warm waves of sensation traveled through her body, throwing her emotions off balance.

"Please, Mademoiselle Martin, come in and be seated."

"Thank you, but before I do, I have a favor to ask."

"I'll leave the door open," he murmured dryly.

She fought another retort. "I thought you accepted my apology."

A faint smile hovered around his lips, without the ice this time. "So I did. What's the favor?"

"I don't want anyone at Ferriers to know I'm here. Could you tell your assistant and the security guard at the main entrance to keep absolutely quiet about this visit?"

After a moment of reflection he nodded. "*Bien sûr.* I'll take care of it now."

While he was gone, she walked across the oriental rug and sat down on one of two blue striped silk love seats facing each other around a coffee table. The couch was upholstered in a blue and white toile she found part of the charm of the elegant room.

Jasmine heard the doors close behind her, sealing them inside.

He rejoined her, cocking his dark head. "Now you don't have to worry. Would you care for tea or coffee? Perhaps a soft drink?"

"Nothing, thank you."

They were circling each other, metaphorically speaking, trying to size each other up. He took a hand out of his pocket and sat in the chair opposite her. Both hands were ringless.

"Congratulations on your new position as head of the Ferrier Corporation. I dare say you're the most famous CEO in modern French history at the moment." The wryness of his tone wasn't lost on her.

One thing she already knew about him. He was a man who spoke his mind. She didn't know if that boded well or not for the shock he was about to receive.

"Thank you, except that I won't be the head for much longer."

"I can't say I'm surprised," he came back with urbane sophistication. "Please don't misunderstand me, but after the introduction on television about your lack of experience and work record, I gather the board is having difficulty following your grandfather's wishes, no matter that you were his personal choice of successor."

Jasmine hadn't seen that assessment coming so fast. It was *her* jaw that went slack, not his. But she couldn't take offense. He was discussing hard business facts and understood how things worked at the top. A shudder went through her to realize he wasn't the president of the bank for nothing. Her uphill battle had already begun.

"Yes," she admitted. "Giles LeClos has called

another board meeting in two weeks for a vote. It doesn't leave me much time to accomplish what has to be done. That's why it was urgent that I see you today if I could. I appreciate your being willing to meet with me without any advance notice."

Her words brought his well-honed body forward. "Surely you must realize that your company's association with our bank over the years means you have instant access, if necessary. I'm glad you came in this morning. This afternoon I'll be out of the city on business, so it's providential that I was still available for this emergency meeting."

"That's what it is, and I'm very grateful." She bit her lip. "First of all, this has to be between the two of us and no one else. I realize you've been meeting with Giles LeClos, who's been in charge since Papa's death. But he mustn't know I've been here or he'll misunderstand and believe I've gone behind his back. In time, he'll be told, but not yet. Will you give me your promise on that?"

He sat back, examining her face with an intensity that made her feel he could see inside her soul. "Go on."

She had to take that as a yes. "Look—there's no point beating around the bush. My grandfather's company has been mismanaged since his death and now it's in huge trouble. No one is more aware of it than you. I intend to save it, but I'm going to need your help."

"You mean in two weeks you plan to pull it out of the red?" Granted his tone was incredulous, not mocking. "Isn't that a little ambitious, even if you have Maxim Ferrier's nose?" She winced. "I realize that sounds cruel, but you've never run a corporation and the bank has continued to extend your loan until it's at the limit."

"I'm very aware of that."

"Then you have to know there's nothing more we can do for you." He shook his head. "Perhaps another bank might be willing to underwrite a second loan for you, but it wouldn't be a wise business decision. Aside from the fact that your revenues are diminishing with little hope of recouping, there's no one at the head who instills enough confidence for the banking board to take a financial risk. Please don't take that as a personal attack against you."

"I won't. I didn't! If I were sitting on the board, I'd have little faith in me too. An empty-headed cliff-jumper who doesn't have a clue about business and is so spoiled by millions of dollars she wouldn't recognize a paycheck if she saw one doesn't exactly fill the bill. Right?"

"Again, those are your words, not mine."

Nothing appeared to faze him. "I believe you. But before you show me the door, I was hoping for the sake of the partnership that has lasted ninety years between your bank and Ferriers, you could find some time to let me make a proposition to you."

His eyes *did* flare at that remark, letting her know she actually had surprised him.

"Not the kind you're thinking, if you were thinking it," she added. "There's a matter of great urgency I need to discuss with you, but it will take some time. We can't do it now when you're already pressed to leave your office on other business. Could you possibly come tomorrow or Friday to my grandfather's laboratory in Grasse? This is vital, or I wouldn't ask."

Jasmine held her breath and prayed while she waited for his answer. She could hear his mind working.

"It would have to be late Friday afternoon. Four-thirty, maybe five. I could give you a half hour, then I have other plans."

Relief flooded her system. "Thank you for being willing to meet me halfway. It's more than I deserve." Jasmine got to her feet. "The lab is the little building on the south side of the perfumery. Just ring me when you're there and I'll let you in." She handed him a piece of paper with her phone number on it. *"À bientôt."*

At four on Friday, Luc left his office and headed for Grasse in his car. Half a dozen times in the last two days he'd reached for his phone to call her and cancel. Each time, he'd get so close, but then he couldn't follow through. The tell-tale throb in her voice when she'd said it was a matter of great urgency kept nagging at him until he couldn't sleep.

He was a fool to meet with her. It gave her hope when there wasn't any. But as she'd said, for the sake of the business both companies had done together over the years, he'd be churlish not to accommodate this one request. His grandfather had revered Maxim Ferrier and would probably have gone the extra mile before he had to turn his granddaughter down. Luc could at least do the same.

Keep on believing that lie, Charriere. You know damn well why you're breaking the speed limit to get there.

In a few minutes, he took the turnoff for the perfumery and wound around to the south side, where he saw the lab and a red Audi parked in front of it. He'd programmed her number into his phone so he wouldn't lose it. When he called her, she answered on the third ring.

"*Bon après-midi, monsieur.* I can't tell you what you coming here means to me." Her comment sounded heartfelt. He honestly didn't know what to make of her. "Every time my phone has rung, I've been afraid it was you calling to cancel because you'd thought the better of it." If only she knew. He got out of the car and walked over to the entrance. "I'm opening the door now."

He heard the sound of the electronic lock and there she was clad in a long-sleeved white lab coat that couldn't camouflage her gorgeous figure. The stains on it looked fresh. "Come in."

There were a few windows open at the very top of the room, but it was semi-dark. This was Maxim Ferrier's inner sanctum. It smelled and felt like Luc had just stepped into an old-school chemistry lab with all its paraphernalia from the nineteen-fifties. There was a worktable in the center of the room. Three walls of stacked shelves with fascinating bottles surrounded them, just as they'd appeared on TV.

She indicated an upholstered swivel chair, the only concession to modern-day décor. It was placed in front of an old oak desk pushed against the wall, piled high with notebooks.

Above it were two framed diplomas, both issued from the Department of Chemistry at the Sorbonne in Paris. The older, yellowing one had the name Maxim Tricornot Valmy Ferrier printed on it. The more recent white diploma displayed the name Jasmine Ferrier Martin. There was a ribbon attached beneath the glass that read, *With honors.*

He swallowed hard when he realized what it meant. No one with an empty head received credentials like that.

"I had two reasons for bringing you here. First, I wanted you to see where I work while I disabuse you of a few false notions about me. I *have* been working for years, but always alongside my papa behind the scenes when I wasn't at university. He paid my salary by putting money into a fund on a regular basis so I could draw from it. Please—sit down, Monsieur Charriere."

"Luc," came his quiet response.

"Luc," she amended. "I dislike formality too. Call me Jasmine. I'd prefer it."

He eyed her soberly. "This is where I eat crow, I presume."

"You're wrong. This is *not* payback time. I'm in deadly earnest when I say I need your help. If I can create a setting where you will really listen and not rush to judgment, that's all I ask. When you've heard me out, if you still can't see a way, then I won't ask again."

"Fair enough," he muttered.

"Thank you." She took a deep breath. "When you and I collided on Yeronisos island, I'd caught a ride in one of the dinghies with those teenagers so I wouldn't have to drive out there alone. My reason for being there was to take some pictures of the excavations.

"I've never been cliff jumping or anything dangerous like that in my life and never will. I too thought those guys were foolish and worried that something could happen, which it did."

Luc was eating a lot of crow by now.

"My grandmother's book was coming out

again the day after my twenty-sixth birthday. She was an amateur archaeologist and had written a section about their travels. She'd lost the pictures she and Papa took together on Yeronisos island, so naturally they hadn't been included in the first edition.

"That's why I went out there and took some in order for them to be included in the second edition. She and Papa had gone there looking for Cleopatra's tomb. The location of that tomb somewhere near Alexandria still remains unknown."

"I know," he ground out. "I've tried looking for it myself."

"*That's* why you were there that day! I wondered."

It was all making sense. "I have an interest in Egyptian archaeology. After doing business in Nicosia, I went out there for the morning before I had to get back to Nice. I thought maybe she and Mark Antony had been buried on Yeronisos beneath the remains of the temple of Apollo, but I saw no signs of their crypt when I was there."

"I'm afraid it's still a mystery."

Luc darted her a glance. "Little did I know it was the new head of Ferriers who climbed to the top of that cliff like one of those amazing warrior women of the Amazon depicted in the myths of the Greeks. All that was missing were your sandals and the lasso of truth."

"If I'd known that two months later it was you of all people I would need to come begging to, I—"

He eyed her frankly. "You would have reacted the same way."

A smile hovered around her beautiful mouth. "My dad and brothers taught me early how to defend myself."

"Tell them they succeeded admirably. It hurts to admit I was impressed how well you protected yourself. You halfway got me believing I was a lech."

She was more of a mystery to him than ever. He'd seen the expert way she'd handled the anchorman—disarming him completely instead of the other way around. Michel Didier hadn't seen it coming either when she'd shot him down for asking a question about her love life.

Jasmine Martin wasn't Maxim Ferrier's granddaughter for nothing. Luc had a feeling she'd inherited her grandfather's shrewd business sense after all, or he would never have chosen her to be at its head.

He watched her pace the floor for a minute before she looked at him. "It's true I don't have years of experience behind me, but I have something else that didn't come out during the TV segment. My grandfather's full confidence."

Luc was listening. "You made that clear during the interview."

"Except that what you heard has little to do with why he named me to head the company. It wasn't because I inherited his nose. Incidentally, mine is nothing like his. There's only one Mozart born in this world. The truth is, Papa needed me to do something he couldn't do while he was alive."

At this point she had Luc so baffled and intrigued at the same time he grew restless and got to his feet. "Go on."

"Forgive me if I'm taking a long time to get to the point, but it's necessary so you'll understand. My grandparents had two homes. A ranch in Idaho in the U.S., where my grandmother was born. The other was the Ferrier family home in Grasse. They raised four children, two boys, two girls, all of whom are on the board except my mother, who was the youngest.

"She grew up loving the ranch and had little interest in being a part of the family perfuming business. She ended up marrying my dad, an Idaho cowboy who had his own ranch close by. My elder brother lives in the original ranch house. My other brother built a home on the same property. We're all just one happy family."

"Am I to assume that explains your strange comment about the 'Frenchman'?" Luc surmised.

"Let's put it this way. American men are very different than Frenchmen, and I've known two Frenchmen who haven't ingratiated themselves to me, thus the comment I made to you. But getting back to the point, I was my parents' third and last child, born on the ranch. My older brothers and I loved our life there, but every time our family traveled to Grasse to visit our grandparents, I found myself snooping around this laboratory and all Papa's stuff.

"If ever my parents or grandmother couldn't find me, I was with him, smelling all the slips he prepared. I loved doing what he did. No dollhouses and tea sets for me. This lab became my own tree house, so to speak.

"I loved it when he'd take me walking with him in the early evenings. He said it was a perfect time to smell the fragrance in the air. During those times he'd tell me he was creating a new perfume. I'd try to create one too and he gave me ideas. I was entranced.

"We used to play a game. He'd test me to find out if I knew what essential oil or chemical he was using. I'd stay up half the night in my bedroom at his house with all his used slips. I would study everything so I'd be ready for his questions the next day."

Luc was entranced by all this too.

"By the time I was twelve, I begged my parents to let me stay with my grandparents for the next nine months and go to school here. My mom adored them and understood how much I loved to be with them. To my joy, she and dad allowed it, but they said I could only do it that one time because they'd miss me too much otherwise. At the time I didn't understand the great sacrifice they made to let me live with my grandparents.

"Before I had to go back home the next June, Papa picked me up and put me on this table I'm leaning against." She patted it. By now she'd mesmerized Luc. "That's when he told me I had the nose.

"But he said I had to keep it a secret. When I turned twenty-six, he would put me in charge of the company. But if he died before that birthday, he would leave instructions that the board install me as the official head after I came of age. In the meantime, he encouraged me to stick by him whenever I could.

"I thought he was kidding at making me the head of the company. I didn't believe he really meant those words. I hardly understood them, but he made me feel special and I adored him. I ended up staying with my grandparents in the summers and during holidays. He let me hover at his side and taught me how to cook up a perfume recipe.

"I met the people he worked with, the farmers, the workers at the distilleries, the workers at the warehouses. He took me on trips with him and grandma to Morocco and India and Nicosia. He taught me the difference between the soils in those climates, and the soil in Grasse, where the sweetest flowers are grown. We also spent time looking at ancient artifacts wherever we went. I couldn't get enough.

"After college in Paris, he asked me to come back to Grasse and work with him in here. Just the two of us. No one else was ever allowed inside. It was during that time he started confiding in me about certain issues in his life that had plagued him since childhood. I learned devastating things that broke my heart.

"Before his death, he asked a great favor of me. He'd devised a plan to remedy his pain, but it needed my help to execute and couldn't be carried out until he died." Her eyes filled with tears. She stopped talking for a minute and stared at him. "This is where you come in, Luc."

Was she playing him?

Unbelievably his cell rang just then. He checked the caller ID. His mother was phoning. They'd just returned from the Orient and his sister had planned a big family party. "Excuse me for a moment, Jasmine. I have to take this."

"Of course."

He walked over to a corner and picked up. "Maman?"

"The party started an hour ago. Where are you? Everyone's waiting!"

"I'll be there in a half hour."

"That long?"

"I had business. It couldn't be helped. See you soon." He clicked off and turned to Jasmine, haunted by more questions that needed answers.

"You gave me an hour," she said, reading his mind. "I understand you have to go, but I haven't come to the most important part yet. Could I meet you at your office next week when it's convenient so we can finish this conversation? You need to hear about the great injustice that has been done. I must have help to solve it. Hopefully *your* help."

Must?

Looking into those fabulous blue orbs of hers, he realized it wasn't just her company that was in trouble. Otherwise he wouldn't have caved and said, "I'll tell my assistant to put you down for eleven a.m. on Monday morning." *Get this over as soon as possible, Charriere.*

CHAPTER THREE

ON SATURDAY MORNING the flower market in Grasse brought hundreds of tourists and natives flocking, Jasmine among them. She waited until she saw the truck from the Fleury flower farm make their delivery. As soon as it was unloaded, she hurried over to the stand and bought a tub full of violets she arranged to have loaded in her car.

With time of the essence, she hurried back to the laboratory to prepare a fresh batch of the recipe she'd been perfecting for over a year. The older batch had passed all her tests and she'd had amazing results when she'd worn the perfume out in public.

But this batch would contain the essential oil that came from this new strain of violet that hadn't been available until very recently. It produced the sweetest scent she'd ever smelled. The difference between the old and new strain of violet was so significant, she literally danced for joy through the next two days while she cooked up her recipe.

By Sunday night, she'd prepared two dozen little bottles of samples, hardly able to wait to give them out.

While she wrote notes in her ledger, she paused. "Papa? I wish you were here to smell this. I'm going to try it out on Lucien Charriere. Tomorrow is my chance to win him over to your plan. If he bites, then the second part of it can get under way.

"But I got off to such a bad start with him I don't know what to think. He has every right to consider me a lightweight. In fact it's a miracle he agreed to come to the lab on Friday. Wish me luck."

As she was locking up the lab, she received another call from Giles. But she had nothing to say to him yet, so she'd been putting him off and would continue to do so until after she'd met with Luc tomorrow. If nothing came of their meeting, then she needed to find another banker, even if Luc had explained she probably wouldn't be successful. At some point, she'd get back to Giles, who no doubt wanted to be sure she'd cleared her calendar to be at the next board meeting when they voted her down.

On her way out to the car with one of her new samples, she saw that Fabrice Guillard, one of the chemists who worked at the perfumery, was waiting for her in his Peugeot.

"*Salut*, Fabrice. What are you doing here on a Sunday night?"

"Lying in wait for you," he said in a seductive voice.

She laughed. If she could believe him, then she wished Luc were here to witness the irony of the situation. But she had an idea someone on the board, possibly Giles, wanted to know what she was up to and had encouraged Fabrice to ask her out. If they were trying to find information that could fortify their claim that she wasn't the best choice to be CEO, they were using the wrong person to do it.

Fabrice pretended to be wounded. "You hurt me, *mademoiselle*. I saw your car and hoped I could take you out for a bite to eat." The attractive, divorced Frenchman with the light brown hair and eyes had recently been brought into the company and was all the talk among the females at the perfumery.

But like André Malroix, a former boyfriend of Jasmine's, and a lot of French men, Fabrice had that ability to chat her up in a seductive way, causing her to believe she was the most beautiful woman on earth. Jasmine had fallen for it until André showed his true colors. She didn't know Fabrice's true colors and didn't want to know because he seemed like the same type. His intimate way of talking irritated her and she wasn't in the mood.

"Thank you for asking, but I have other plans. My advice for you is to wait for one of the girls after work tomorrow. I can promise you'll have better luck with Suzette. I heard she finds you intelligent and fun to be around."

"*Oh, là là.* I think you're afraid of men, *chérie.*"

"If you're talking French men, you're absolutely right."

"Why do you say that?"

If he got her going on her list, they'd be out here all night. If he was innocent of an agenda and only wanted to be with her, it still didn't matter. "I don't think you want to know. Have a lovely evening, Fabrice. *Ciao.*"

Even though Luc had braced himself for his eleven o'clock appointment, Jasmine Martin's appearance in the doorway of his office had managed to upend him until he was reeling from sensation after sensation. While he watched her take a seat, the mold of her body did amazing things for her summery print skirt and blouse in blues and greens on white. With legs that went on and on and a mouth that was temptation itself, how in the hell was he going to focus?

The buzz from the intercom drove him across the room to his desk. Thomas wouldn't have bothered him if it weren't important. He picked up his phone. *"Oui?"*

"You've had three calls, all urgent. Now Monsieur LeClos is on the line and says it's vital he get in touch with you today."

With two years of diminishing earnings reports, things were getting hotter at Ferriers. Luc knew LeClos wanted another extension of their existing loan and was going behind Jasmine's back.

He darted her a glance, then checked his watch. "Tell everyone I'm in conference and will return calls after three, no sooner. In the meantime, Ms. Martin and I will need lunch brought in. With that exception, I don't want to be disturbed."

"Très bien."

After hanging up, he turned to her and rested against the edge of his desk with his hands braced on either side. "Let's start with my visit to your lab on Friday. You stated at the time that you'd asked me to meet you there for two reasons. After eating crow, I never heard the second reason."

She re-crossed her elegant legs. "If you hadn't had to leave, I would have told you."

"Well, I'm not going anywhere now. The time is yours to explain. You made a comment on Friday when you said that you *must* have my help to solve a great injustice. That sounded cryptic and quite a different matter from the fact that your company is in arrears on your loan payment. Why don't you begin by telling me about this injustice. Against whom?"

Her hands went to the arms of the chair. She stared into his eyes without wavering. "Against the rightful heir to the company."

"Rightful heir?" Maybe he hadn't heard her correctly. "In principle, all of you Ferriers are heirs."

She nodded, drawing his attention to her glistening dark sable hair. "That's true. All the Ferriers born to my grandparents are Papa's heirs. But Papa wasn't the legitimate heir to the Ferrier dynasty. Ferrier wasn't even Papa's legal name. Not in the beginning."

Dumbfounded, Luc walked toward her. "What was it?"

"Tricornot."

First the revelations during the television interview that had knocked him sideways. Now this... "Who *is* the real heir?"

"Papa's cousin, Remy Ferrier."

At this point, Luc was confused. "According to the media from years ago, he was the wealthy no-account alcoholic who crashed one sports car after another. I heard he was a womanizer who failed at several marriages and a race car business, then went off somewhere never to be heard of again. You're telling me *he's* the real heir?"

Whatever he'd said caused her to jump out of the chair and start pacing. He'd obviously offended her. "I'm sorry, Jasmine. I was only repeating the gossip that circulated when I was a younger man."

She finally stopped pacing and turned to him. "Remy was a good-looking man who attracted women in droves with or without his money. He never knew if they loved him for himself or not.

"Yes, he did love fast cars and he did crash quite a few of them because he loved speed and should have raced in the Grand Prix with his friend Marcello. He was that good. When he realized he was getting too old to race, he designed a revolutionary race car, but the business he tried to establish along with it failed because he couldn't find enough backers."

"But he had millions."

"No. He had nothing! His father cut off his funds. His one marriage failed, and yes, he drank too much. But that isn't who Remy really is." A world of sadness had entered those blue eyes.

"Is he still alive?"

"Very much so and living in Grasse."

"You're kidding—I don't understand. Why hasn't anyone heard about him in all these years?"

"Because he's been quietly working on his own flower farm, which is thriving."

"Flower farm?" Lines marred Luc's features. "And yet he's not associated with your family's perfume business?"

Her lovely jaw hardened. "No. But once upon a time Remy *was* the business, the *integral* part," she emphasized to the point that it raised hairs on the back of his neck. "But his birthright was stolen and given to another."

"Stolen?" Luc was confounded by what she was telling him.

She nodded and sat back down again. "On behalf of my papa, I've come to you. He despised being the head of the company and never wanted any part of that aspect or the fame. I'm here to make certain Remy attains his rightful place at last. With a loan from you, I can make that happen."

A loan, he mouthed. "We've already had this

discussion, Jasmine. Are you talking about another loan for you personally?"

"For me, for Remy, for Papa, for the very preservation of the company. That's why I've continued to darken your doorstep."

Darken was hardly the word, but the revelations continually pouring out of her had him stymied. "Are you talking a real Jacob and Esau story here?"

"In a way."

"Explain the twist to me."

"The culprit wasn't Remy or my grandfather."

"Then all the accolades heaped on your grandfather are still true?"

"Of course. Just as all the ugliness about Remy's supposedly profligate life was the work of someone as close to a monster as you can get."

Luc rubbed his lower lip with his thumb. "Who would that be?"

"Remy's father."

More confused, he shook his head. "You mean the brother of Paul Ferrier? I don't remember his name."

Her gaze held his. "Gaston was Paul's brother. But Remy's father was Paul Ferrier, the tyrannical head of Ferriers all those years."

"What?"

The things she was saying now were even more astounding than her announcement that she was Maxim Ferrier's granddaughter. While he was attempting to sort out all this new information, there was a tap on the door.

Luc walked to the entrance and took the tray of sandwiches and salad from his assistant. "Remember," he murmured. "No disturbance now, no mention of who's inside my office. One slip and you're fired."

Thomas went stone-cold sober. "I swear I won't say a word," he promised before closing the door.

Luc walked back to the table and lowered the tray. Jasmine looked up. "Thank you for lunch."

"I'm hungry too. Join me."

She reached for a half sandwich and coffee before settling back in the chair. He fixed himself a plate and sat down. "Whenever you're ready,

I'd like to hear this amazing tale from the definitive source."

"That's *moi*." Her head flew back, unsettling the hair sweeping her shoulders. Her comment had come out solemn rather than teasing.

"Papa's father was a Tricornot, his mother a Valmy."

Luc made a sound. "I remember seeing those names on your grandfather's diploma."

"Yes. They died, so he was adopted by his mother's sister, Dominique. She was married to Gaston Ferrier. They couldn't have children so they gave Papa their last name. But the situation was doomed at the outset because the three of them lived in the family home in Grasse with Gaston's brother, Paul Ferrier, his wife, Rosaline, and their son, Remy."

Luc poured himself some coffee. "How did they all stand to live together?"

"For Papa and Remy, it was a natural phenomenon because they didn't know anything else. But it was on Paul's insistence they lived together in order to keep the perfume recipes from falling into the wrong hands. He was a tyrant and it was his way of controlling everything to ensure the family business secrets stayed hidden from the rest of the world.

"Paul had a nose, but not a good one by anyone's standards. Gaston tried to take care of the business, but was in fragile health. From the very beginning it was Remy who did the flower farming and virtually ran the whole business from distillation to marketing. Remy had that special gift to know the precise moment when to harvest, when to cut the flowers and prepare them for enfleurage.

"He knew every inch of ground, every flower, the seasons, the farmers he worked with, the demands of the market. Without Remy, Ferriers would never have become a great operation. But Paul destroyed his own son in the process."

Totally intrigued he asked, "In what way?"

"Remy didn't have the nose. The family discovered that Papa did."

"How did that happen?"

"While Papa was fiddling around in the perfumery laboratory, he found some discarded slips of paper with different scents on them. To Gaston's great astonishment, Papa could identify some of the various oils."

"Exactly what happened to you!"

"Yes. Both families were stunned. The normal person can pick out three, maybe four components. A *nose* can detect a mixture of a hundred or more ingredients in their precise amounts, and blindfolded, pick out the various scents from the essential oils that contribute to a recipe. Even as a child, Papa exhibited this extraordinary gift to a much greater degree than anyone dreamed, including Paul."

"But if Maxim wasn't Paul's son, then how did he inherit his ability to create perfume? He couldn't have gotten it from his birth or adoptive parents." Luc reached for another sandwich, completely engrossed.

She shook her head. "There's no explanation as to why one person has the gift and another does not. By some inexplicable reason, Papa was gifted. And he was the only nose in the

Ferrier family dating back ninety years who didn't have a Ferrier gene in him."

"But he had the genius to create scents." Luc was finally getting the picture. "Fascinating since he had the greatest nose this generation has seen. So the true Ferrier was replaced by the adoptive son."

"More than replaced!" she cried. "Paul idolized him, gave him everything...his time, his possessions. He ignored his own wife, who by then was in a wheelchair. Papa became his *raison d'être*. Remy was virtually invisible to his father. Paul Ferrier was a terrible, terrible man." Her voice shook. "He kept Remy tied to him to do the work, not giving him time off to race cars in the seasonal rallies with his Italian racing friend, Marcello. Remy was his father's slave."

"That's the worst story of its kind I've ever heard," Luc murmured emotionally. He was pained for people he didn't even know.

"You don't know the half of it. Remy's mother begged him to leave and make a different life for himself, but he loved Rosaline and wouldn't leave her in her crippled condition from arthritis. Paul forgot his wife and son existed."

Tears escaped her eyes. "You can't imagine how this killed my grandfather. It was all so unfair. To think he was set on the exalted Ferrier throne because he'd been blessed with a very keen olfactory sense, and Remy was not. Papa loved Remy, Luc!" she cried.

"He grieved over the situation and knew Remy was the greatest flower farmer in the South of France, that he ran everything seamlessly and should always have been at the head. When Remy turned twenty-nine, Paul cut off all money that should have gone to his son, money Remy had earned. Six months later Paul died.

"As soon as he passed way, Papa begged him to come back to Grasse and take over the business. But by then Remy was in a bad way and refused to talk to anyone. Papa heard he was in Paris trying to build a race car business. He sent him money through Marcello to help him get started, but Remy never touched it.

"Papa begged him to come back and run the whole company, but Remy's pride wouldn't allow him to go there. Too much damage had been done. All these years Papa has kept in touch with Marcello, begging him to talk to Remy for him and get him to come home. But Remy couldn't do it."

Luc knew there had to be a lot more to the story than she was telling, but he let it go for now.

"Remy had started drinking heavily by then and his business failed. Later on, he married and they had a son, but their marriage fell apart. His wife left him because there was no money, but his son stuck by him. They came back to the house and small property Remy's mother had left him. He began flower farming again, but he's had no contact with the family."

She wiped her eyes. "Papa had to live with that sorrow for the rest of his life. I became his confidant. Papa put me in charge because he expected me to fix what he couldn't while he was alive.

"He hated the honors Paul bestowed upon him. All he'd wanted was to create perfume. Remy should have run the empire. This ate Papa alive. Behind all the success, both their lives were a giant sore that never healed because Paul forgot Remy even existed."

A shuddering breath came out of her. "Papa developed a plan to restore Remy's birthright and change the map for the future betterment of the company as soon as I was put in charge. With your help, I can give Remy back his dignity and set him up to run Ferriers the way he should have been able to do years ago. He'll make it greater than it has ever been.

"But because of his wounded pride, Remy will never accept the position unless he feels he has something vital to contribute." Her eyes implored him. "So I've come to you for the loan that will accomplish the miracle."

Luc couldn't have foreseen this coming, not in a million years. He was still trying to grasp the enormity of the Ferrier family tragedy.

"You have to understand Remy has a great

business mind. Papa wanted him installed so he can run the show as only he knows how to do. Once, when Papa went to South America for six weeks, Remy was put in charge and went to Paris. He ran the company without a hitch and brought in new accounts without effort."

Once.

"I know what you're thinking. But when Papa asked him to do it, he did it flawlessly."

Luc closed his eyes for a minute while he digested what she was asking.

"Remy's brilliant, Luc. So's his scientist son, Jean-Louis, who runs his own firm in the Sophia Antipolis complex here in Nice and is helping Remy. Today he sells the harvest from his crops independently. The kind of crop he's been cultivating could bring millions of dollars to the family business if he had the money to buy up more property to grow more crops. I know where to lay hands on the kind of land he needs.

"I have the figures worked out to show how we can recoup our losses. Papa kept the business on top as best he could, but since his death, one bad decision after another has been made. Everything's here on paper." She got up and handed him the folder she'd brought in.

Jasmine had pled her case and had won him over emotionally without showing him anything. But financially, all the negatives against the idea had been stacking up. "How old is he?"

"Sixty-six."

Ciel! That was old for the bank to go with a supposed recovered alcoholic. Maxim Ferrier couldn't honestly have believed his cousin could take on the whole board at Ferriers and gain their trust. Certainly Luc's bank wouldn't consider it, no matter that his pipe dream was well meant.

"Through my sources I know he stopped drinking a long time ago," Jasmine read his mind. "He lives with his son and his wife and their children."

Luc shook his head. Granting another loan of the size she was talking about meant taking a huge risk, one his bank couldn't afford. Though he could pass this by the banking board of directors, to win a nod would take a miracle. Everything was against it. *He* was still against it for the obvious reasons.

She unexpectedly got up from the chair. "If I have to, I'll put up the family home and the property surrounding it for collateral."

Mon Dieu. For her to risk losing such a personal legacy was unfathomable to him. Clearly she was in this for the fight of her life, and it would be a fight. But he had to admire her because she was willing to risk everything by taking the moral high ground. All for the sake of the true son.

"I can read your mind, Luc. You think it would be a risk to loan more money, but there's a saying: to win without risk is to triumph without glory. You'd be doing a great thing. Please remember something else. I came to you first. If you decide we can't do business, I'll go elsewhere until I find the right banker. This isn't a threat. I'm just being practical and I'm in a hurry."

She got up from the chair, but he grasped her

arm before she could leave. She spun around in surprise. "Don't go out that way, Jasmine. Use my private entrance so no one in the bank will see you leave."

Her eyes flashed a midnight blue as she eased her arm from his grasp. "That's all right. I've asked too big a favor already."

A pretty impossible favor. One he couldn't see himself granting. "I'm sorry, but in all honesty I don't believe the banking board will be willing to do business with you under such circumstances."

"In other words, the answer is no."

"I'm afraid so. But please—let me walk you out."

Without taking no for an answer, he headed for his private entrance. Together they left via the rear exit. He followed her to the Audi she'd parked around the side. After she'd climbed behind the wheel, accidentally giving him a brief glimpse of her gorgeous legs where the material rode up her thigh, she lowered the window.

He put a hand on top of the car and leaned toward her. "Just a minute," he said, causing her to pause. "Before you leave, what's that scent you're wearing? It's sweet and fresh, like the way spring smells."

"It doesn't have a name."

"You mean it's a recipe you just cooked up for the fun of it," he teased, remembering her comment from the broadcast.

A faint smile hovered at the corner of her mouth. He really was in trouble now. "Something like that."

Luc studied the shape of it longer than he should have. "Promise you won't think I'm playing up to your good side if I tell you I like it more than anything I've ever smelled on a woman?"

Her smile deepened. "I believe you. Do you know I get that same response from almost every man I meet or work with? I've been wearing it off and on for a year now. What you're responding to is the pure scent of the Parma violet."

"Violet? So that's what it is! I couldn't put my finger on it."

"They've all but disappeared, that's why."

He frowned. "What happened?"

"In the nineteenth century around Grasse there were large plantings being grown for the perfume industry. Sadly in the eighteen-nineties a synthetic violet fragrance was discovered and was soon manufactured cheaply, putting an end to the production of the natural oil.

"But Remy has brought the Parma violet back to Grasse from Italy. Over the last few years he's spent his time cultivating it and perfecting several unique varieties for their scent. His best one comes from a cultivar with a very strong constitution. When he can plant more, it's going to create a brand new niche that's been missing in the Ferrier perfume market."

"And what is that?" Luc asked. He'd never met such an incredible woman.

"A scent men *like* to smell on a woman. In general, women dress and buy scents to suit themselves."

A scent men like to smell...

Yes...they did. *He* did.

The novel marketing idea blew him away. So did her vast knowledge, which continued to humble him.

"Paul Ferrier had no clue his son was a genius. He considered him baggage." Luc grimaced to think a father could do that to a son. "With the help of Jean-Louis, Remy has developed a secret weapon that will soon put Ferriers in the black again. You were my first choice for a backer, but I'll find another to get him what he needs. Mark my words."

She put on her sunglasses. "I realize I'm lucky you didn't throw me out after I barged in last week. For you to feed me just now tells me why Papa dealt with your bank exclusively over the years."

With that comment, she turned on the engine and started to back out. Before leaving the parking area she waved to him. "You summed me up in a big hurry on Yeronisos island, so I don't know why I expected anything else from you in regard to Remy Ferrier. But I thank you for your time and for being up-front so no more time is wasted. *Au revoir, monsieur.*"

At the end of Luc's work day, he took the chance that his friend Nic hadn't gone home from work yet, and drove to his office in the technopole research park of Sophia Antipolis. He wound around the pine-covered hills to reach Valfort Technologies.

Not that long ago Luc had participated in a massive four-day search of the park with police dogs, hoping to discover the remains of Nic's first wife, who'd been missing for three years. Miraculously, her body had been found and it had been discovered she'd been shot and buried in the heavily wooded area. What had been meant to be a kidnapping had turned out to be a murder. Only a man with Nic's strength could have gotten through such a horrendous ordeal.

Every time Luc came here, he was reminded of his friend's pain, but the knowledge that Nic had found love again drove away the darkness.

Luc needed to talk, and there was no one who listened better than Nic.

Monday evening wasn't the greatest time to drop by, but Luc decided to take a chance anyway. Robert, Nic's assistant, smiled when Luc stepped inside. "I'll let Nic know you're here."

"Is he with a client?"

"No. He's through for the day. This is a good time."

A minute later, his dark-haired friend, sporting a new tan, invited him into his office with a bear hug and shut the door. "It's good to see you! Sit down. Want a soda? Coffee?"

"Nothing right now. I called last week to see if you could go deep-sea fishing and found out you were on a trip to California. Looks like it agreed with you."

"We had a great time, but I have to admit I'm glad to be back." Nic was a new man since his marriage. Luc hardly recognized him. "Laura and I were just talking about getting you and Yves together for dinner on Saturday night at our house. Are you still seeing Gabrielle?"

"No. That was over weeks ago."

His friend perched on the corner of his desk. "That settles that. Something's wrong. What is it?"

"I've met a woman."

A chuckle escaped Nic. "Since they throw themselves at you, I'm not surprised."

Luc shook his head. "This one is different."

"In what way?"

"In ways even you can't imagine."

"You mean you're interested for the first time since—"

"Yes," Luc cut him off. "But it's much more than that."

Nic started to smile. "Are you saying what I think you're saying?"

He raked a hand through his hair. "I don't know. I'm in trouble, Nic. Real trouble. Do you have time to talk?"

"After the years you put up listening to me talk through my pain, you know I've got time. First of all, who is she?"

Luc couldn't stay seated. He walked around

for a minute. "Did you happen to see the news on TV about the new head of the Ferrier Corporation?"

"Who didn't? I think every male watching on six continents was blown away by the gorgeous granddaughter of Maxim Ferrier." When Luc didn't comment, Nic eyed him in disbelief. "*She's* the woman?"

He nodded. "Jasmine Martin."

Nic let out a whistle. "How long has this been going on?"

"Since a week ago Friday, but we met two months before that when I went to Nicosia on business. We ran into each other on Yeronisos island."

"Literally?" He grinned.

"Not exactly. But that's a whole story in itself."

"Does she feel the same way about you?"

Luc rubbed the back of his neck. "I don't know what she feels."

"How could you not know something like that?"

"It's complicated. She came to me for a loan."

"*Eh bien, mon ami.* Why don't you start at the beginning? I want to hear about what happened on Yeronisos, and then I want to know why a woman who's worth millions of dollars on her own came to you for money."

"I don't think she *is* worth millions or she wouldn't have said she'd put up the Ferrier personal property for collateral."

A whistle came out of Nic.

For the next half hour, Luc unloaded to the friend he would trust with his life. It felt good to let it all out and try to make sense of it. When he'd finished, he said, "I never saw anyone so invested in another person's happiness. It's been a revelation to me."

"I agree it's a gut-wrenching story," Nic murmured.

"It is, but much as I would have liked to grant her request, I had to turn her down for the loan. Remy Ferrier has too many problems that wouldn't inspire confidence in the banking board." He rubbed his jaw for a minute.

"She mentioned something about Remy's son, who was helping him. Since you work here at the complex, do you happen to know of a Jean-Louis Ferrier? I'm curious. Jasmine said he had an office around here somewhere."

Nic nodded. "I've only met him once. It was after the search for my wife. I stopped by to thank everyone in the complex who'd been a part of it. I learned he's a scientist running a firm in the next section east of me. It seems his team is on the cutting edge of technology for some new miracle processes involving plants and animals. Because of my technological background, I found our conversation fascinating."

Luc sat forward in the chair with his hands clasped between his legs. "I didn't know there was another Ferrier related to Remy here in Nice."

"Small world, isn't it? To my knowledge they're focusing primarily on understanding the cellular mechanisms that underlie the development and physiology of plants and animals, which provides the foundation for biotechnology innovation. From the way he explained it to me, there's this molecular circuit that acts as a bio-timer to control the diverse growth pathways in plants and animals."

Luc took a deep breath. "When Jasmine said Remy was working with his son, I didn't realize what she meant." *Because you didn't give her a chance?*

Nic eyed him thoughtfully. "This discovery allows farmers to save on both man power and shipping, as naturally maturing crops will not all flower at the same time, leading to the less than optimal use of resources. This technique to synchronize the flowering, to maximize the yield or reduce the cost of harvesting, is revolutionary because you can do it all at the same time and potentially reduce wastage.

"If Remy is trying it out with his Parma violets and is having success, then it could revolutionize the flower industry. More harvests in one season could mean additional profits for the farmer."

"So *that* was the secret weapon she'd talked

about," Luc blurted. It seemed he'd jumped to another conclusion too fast without knowing all the facts. Times had changed since Remy ran the company. Luc felt the banking board wouldn't think the sixty-six-year-old farmer was the right person to take over, but Nic's explanation about his son's work had thrown a new light on the situation.

His friend smiled. "Besides being a beauty, she's definitely unique. So tell me what else is wrong."

Luc got to his feet. "I never wanted to feel this way about a woman again."

"Obviously she's into you too."

"There have been moments along the way when I thought— Oh, hell, I don't know. I can't read her yet."

"Give it time, Luc. Once you get past the business part, then you'll be able to explore what could be between you."

"I'm afraid I ruined it when I turned her down for the loan."

Nic stared at him. "Why don't you bring her over on Saturday night so we can meet her?"

"After today, I don't know if she'll ever speak to me again."

"Want to take bets on that?"

Luc's brows lifted. "I'll think about it and let you know," he muttered. "Thanks, Nic. I don't know what I'd do without you."

"That makes two of us."

CHAPTER FOUR

JASMINE'S JAW WENT taut as she headed for the house Tuesday evening. Yesterday she'd given Luc Charriere the grand performance of her life, but it had all been for naught. This was supposed to be the honeymoon phase of her inauguration with the company, but her failure to get Luc on board had come as a crushing blow.

She gripped the steering wheel tighter as she took the exit leading away from the lab, which she'd left early. The thought of walking over to the perfumery and facing Giles's wooden expression, let alone the many phone calls that needed answering, was too daunting.

Good karma hadn't been with her yesterday. Otherwise, the scent she'd been wearing might have made him curious enough to delve into that file she'd left and rethink his position.

Though emotions had welled up inside her and she'd laid it all out, he'd turned her down flat.

When he'd come to the laboratory last week, she'd read those negative signs coming from him, the kind you picked up by osmosis. Part of her understood he had legitimate reasons for making his decision. She'd heard them running through his mind. But she hadn't wanted to accept them.

You're a fool, Jasmine. An imbécile. *Idiote.*

She dashed the tears from her eyes. After the experience on the island, she should have known his answer would be an emphatic no. Shaken by the depth of her intense attraction to him in spite of how things had turned out, she decided to go home and put Luc out of her mind once and for all.

To unwind after her session with the man who'd watched her climb Yeronisos—a spine-tingling thought—she took the long way back to La Tourette, passing the sloping fields of acacia, geranium, tuberose and jasmine blooming beneath the afternoon summer sky.

She scanned the horizon. Her favorite view was of the flowers growing up against the white stucco farmhouses. Beyond them, the rocky promontories knifed skyward. Between the crags, the many little villages of pale cream and red lay in repose. Normally this drive helped her relax, but for some reason she was feeling a new restlessness.

If she were being honest, Lucien Charriere was responsible for it.

That's why she couldn't focus on anything. A new hunger had been aroused in her while she'd poured out her soul to him. His compassion for what he'd heard couldn't be denied. It had been there in his eyes, but he still believed that extending a new loan was a bad business decision and there was nothing she could do about it.

He'd given her all the time she'd needed to state her case when she knew his assistant had to put his other clients off in order to accommodate her. She could still feel his hand on her arm. Her body still throbbed from his touch.

His mention of the scent she was wearing had established an intimacy between them so strong it had raised her pulse.

Tortured by this new sense of yearning to know what his mouth tasted and felt like, she drove on, winding up the steep hillside on the other side of the gorge. He was nothing like the Andrés and Fabrices with whom she'd worked, those who thought they could sweep you off your feet with their specialized love verbiage.

Luc wasn't like any Frenchman she'd met, who, young or old, single, married or divorced, hit on her all the time whether she wore perfume or not. Luc had maintained an aloofness balanced with just the right amount of professional courtesy and interest. How insane was it that he was the only man of her acquaintance to produce this physical response in her. To think about him all the time like this was madness.

Soon, she reached the fieldstone house on the family estate. Long promenades of cypress trees flanked her progress. The smell of the orange trees told her she was close to La Tourette.

The house had emptied of family who'd gathered here the weekend from last, and now were gone. Though she'd wanted them to stay longer, her father's ranching responsibilities meant he needed to get back home.

Jasmine got out of the car and hurried inside. She found Sylvie in the kitchen. "I'm home for the night," she told the housekeeper. "If I want dinner later, I'll fix it myself."

The wiry fifty-year-old Provençale from Aix was a literal dynamo. "I've already put your meal in the fridge whenever you want it."

"Bless you." Jasmine blew her a kiss and disappeared upstairs to her bedroom. She opened the French doors onto the terrace and walked out. Grasse, the queen of the French Riviera, lay below, a sight implanted in her heart. Beyond it shimmered the blue Mediterranean.

When she'd left this room earlier in the day, she'd been Jasmine Martin with an agenda that had consumed her from the moment she'd turned twenty-six and had been made the head of the company. But standing here now, she realized she wasn't that same person anymore. Suddenly she felt like she was teetering on the edge of that cliff in Cyprus, terrified and in pain all at the same time.

How could meeting one man have done this to her so fast? It was insane!

In her world as a chemist, there was an explanation for this phenomenon called flash point. It was the lowest temperature at which a flammable liquid like essential jasmine oil will give off enough vapor to ignite when exposed to flame. Flash point was also the critical stage in some process, event or situation at which action, change or violence occurred.

That's what had happened to her. She'd been at her lowest point when she'd entered the Banque Internationale du Midi. But when she'd discovered Luc there, she'd ignited as if she'd been torched by flame. In that instant, a change had occurred, altering her state. She now stood at this railing a transformed woman, filled with those age-old longings called desire.

Jasmine couldn't believe it had finally happened to her. She'd thought herself impervious. When she'd discussed it with her mother, Blanchette had laughed gently and warned her that the day would come when Jasmine would be overcome by her attraction to a man. Just pray he would be the right kind of male, worthy of her.

Why did it have to be the man she'd clashed with on the island? Why was he the man she needed in her corner? One who had the power to put Remy on the throne at Ferriers. But he had chosen not to, and there wasn't a thing she could do about it.

Jasmine had put all her eggs in one basket by appealing to him first. It had made sense to turn to the banking institution Ferriers had relied on for close to a century. But Luc wasn't his grandfather. He was a savvy modern businessman with modern ideas, a man of today. She should have known deep down he would never let sentiment overrule his good sense and practical thinking.

She'd argued her case on sentiment and lost.

Jasmine needed to prepare a list of other bankers to contact. It was time to move on to her next target and forget she had ever known Luc Charriere.

After changing into jeans and a top, she went downstairs to the den to begin her search. Before she could get busy, her cell phone rang. It could be anyone. Much as she didn't want to talk to a soul right now, she didn't dare ignore it. Maybe it was her family. She had to be sure everything was all right with them.

When she saw Luc's name on the caller ID, she almost dropped the phone. She'd thought she would never hear from him again. *Be as businesslike as possible, Jasmine. Don't let your voice shake.* She clicked on. "Hello?"

"Good evening, Jasmine. Am I calling at a bad time?"

"No. I just got home from work. What can I do for you?"

"Since you left my office yesterday, I've taken another look at your file."

Her pulse thudded off the charts. "Why?"

"I've done a little homework and am curious about this land you mentioned."

What?

"There's no price or description on it. You've indicated nothing about it but its existence. If I were to consider your proposition further, I'd need to know what we're talking about here."

She couldn't believe he'd called her back. She couldn't believe he was still thinking about it. Naturally he wanted to know how much money she needed to borrow, but she had been so convinced there was no hope, this phone call shocked her.

"You did mention you're in a hurry," he said quietly.

She cleared her throat. "Yes."

"Under the circumstances, are you free in the morning to show it to me with the Realtor?"

Jasmine was so thrilled he was willing to go this far, she did a little jump. "Absolutely, but I haven't contacted a Realtor yet. Let's just say I've had inside information and know it's been put on the market."

"Why doesn't that surprise me?" The comment made her smile. "Then if it's all right with you I'll drive to Grasse and you can show me. Where shall we meet?"

Not at the house. She never knew when one of her aunts or uncles might drop by. It was the family home to all of them. Though Jasmine lived there, her grandparents had always said everyone was welcome to come and stay as long as they wanted. Their deaths hadn't changed anything in that regard.

"Do you know the old abandoned abbey on the upper road?"

"*Bien sûr.* Shall we meet there at say nine a.m.?"

"I'll be there. Thank you for at least being curious enough to listen to me."

"I owe it to Ferriers. They've been one of our best clients for decades. *A toute à l'heure.*"

Jasmine heard the click before she was ready to hang up. He'd been cordial just now, but still all business. She no longer felt like jumping.

When she thought about it, he was probably humoring her by being willing to look at the land she had her eye on. As he'd said, this was what a banker did who'd been a friend to the company for so many years, even if he still planned to turn her down.

Tomorrow she'd be all business too and kept telling herself that throughout the night.

When Jasmine awakened the next morning, her bedding was all over the place. She'd had a restless night.

After showering, she dressed in her generic uniform, which consisted of a short-sleeved, light blue blouse and matching cotton skirt. At work, her clothes took a beating even with a lab coat. Once she'd shown Luc the property, she would head directly to the lab.

Relieved to hear from her folks that all was well at home, she fastened her hair at the nape with a matching blue elastic and went down the old black staircase to eat breakfast. On the way, she passed hundreds of small framed photos lining the walls. Remy's mother had arranged them years earlier. The history of the Ferriers was written here, and Remy was prominent in many of them.

Jasmine paused in front of the one she loved best. Remy—ever devoted—was standing in the garden of white Parma violets behind his mom, who was in her wheelchair. She held a bunch of them he'd grown and picked just for her. Jasmine knew the story behind every picture.

Remy and his mother both had dark red hair. In this picture, he was developing into the handsome man he would become.

"Whether Luc helps us or not, you're going to be in charge soon, Remy. Just wait and see."

She removed it from the wall and put it in her large straw bag. Then she rushed the rest of the way to the kitchen to drink a half cup of tea and grab a plum. It earned a frown from Sylvie before she hurried outside to her car parked on the gravel drive.

The same warm-growing-hot morning greeted her, but this day was different from all the others. Her body knew it, otherwise her heart wouldn't be racing. She wished it were only because she needed her plan to work, but that would be a lie.

Jasmine couldn't wait to see Luc Charriere again. All the reasons she shouldn't be interested in a Frenchman she needed to do business with didn't matter. Chemistry had taken over. As a scientist, she knew she couldn't fight it.

The solution would be to avoid him. If, by some miracle, the loan was granted, then Remy would be the one working with him in the future. But if Luc turned her down again, as she suspected he would, then that would put an end to everything and they'd go their separate ways.

To dwell on him was idiotic. She knew nothing about him. Being a Frenchman, he had a lover of course, but he'd be discreet. You couldn't be a French male without one. She knew what the field workers talked about all the time. Women. Jasmine often plopped on a straw hat and helped with the harvest. It was a revelation.

She learned about the ones they'd already been with, the ones they were planning to be with, the ones they were getting tired of. The ones their friends were seeing, the ones they'd stopped seeing, the ones who were stepping out on their husbands, the ones who wanted to step out with them.

Aside from her papa, Jasmine had always preferred American men. They loved women too, but they weren't as open about it. She liked the strong silent cowboy types like Hank Branson, the guy she'd had her first big crush on.

As soon as Remy was installed, she planned to go home and get married. It probably wouldn't be to a cowboy like her father. But that didn't matter. She wanted to get back to the ranch on the other side of the Teton mountain range and prove her love to her family. Jasmine had promised them she'd come back to live. She loved ranching too and longed to start her own family where she could be around her married siblings.

Jasmine was retiring from the world of perfume. Hopefully a grandchild of Remy's would inherit the gift to make up a recipe that would keep Ferriers on top. But that was no longer her concern.

Neither was Luc Charriere, who could never be part of her American dream.

But her body groaned when she drove up to the ruin of the old abbey and found him lounging against a dark green Jaguar convertible with his arms folded. His masculine body filled out his white linen shirt with contrasting buttons to perfection. Her eyes dropped down to his powerful legs covered in beige twill pants. Italian leather sandals completed the picture.

She sighed audibly at the sight of him with that five o'clock shadow. For a minute she was imagining him in a western shirt and a Stetson.

Which was true? The clothes made the man, or the man made the clothes? What a ridiculous question when the evidence stood before her. The *man* made the clothes! At least this man did. With the riddle solved, she got out of her car.

But she bet he'd never ridden a horse. That alone was a huge strike against him.

* * *

The new head of Ferriers didn't dress fit to kill. Spoiled women who came from a background of wealth—and Luc had seen and worked with a lot of them—couldn't spend money fast enough to adorn themselves in the latest designer fashions.

That wasn't the case with this woman. With a face and body like hers, Jasmine Martin didn't need to. She had other tantalizing assets, including a mind and thoughts that were so far removed from the superficiality of this world, he marveled. She moved with the kind of femininity a man enjoyed and was compelled to watch.

"*Bonjour*, Luc. I can't thank you enough for being willing to meet me here. I'll admit I was surprised to hear from you at all."

"*Bonjour*, Jasmine." Since losing sleep over her last night had nothing to do with business, her comment had touched on dangerous ground. "I decided to give more thought to what I read in your file, but—"

"I understand the buts," she interrupted him.

"This is not a commitment from you. If you'll follow me, we'll be there in approximately one minute."

With her suggestion, there was no risk of them being thrown together in the same car where they would be in touching distance. Danger avoided, for the moment.

He gave her a nod and they were off. She drove fast across the dips and crests of the hillside. After winding around a bend, she slowed to a stop beside a field lying fallow. Luc pulled behind her and got out. She hurried toward him.

"Ten days ago, one of my inside sources informed me this land is available again. This is exactly what I've been looking for, but I'd need to move fast."

"Tell me about it."

"The monks farmed this land for years. When the old abbey burned, the property was put on the market. It sat for a long time. The only company with enough money to do something with it wanted to turn the whole place into a subdivision for middle-income housing. For the last year, the owner and would-be buyer have gone the rounds in negotiations, but they fell apart because of public pressure to keep the land free of buildings."

"I'm violently against these hillsides being exploited," he asserted.

Emotion seemed to turn her eyes a darker blue. "You're one of the good guys in the banking business."

"I'm a native Niçois. This land is my home too."

"You sound like Papa. With our perfect climate and soil, both he and Remy lamented seeing these fields sold off to hungry developers. It's a tragedy that the cost of labor and the growth of synthetic perfume components have made flower farming less rewarding. Nowadays many of the perfume houses go to their source of oils in North Africa and India. Papa fought to keep Ferriers from going the same route."

He flashed her a smile. "Now *you've* taken up the flag."

"I'm going to try with everything in me." A

pulse throbbed at the base of her creamy throat. His own pulse picked up her beat.

"How big is this property?"

"We'll have to get the figures from the Realtor, but at one time I understand they had as many as fifty thousand individual plantings of vegetables like carrots, onions, fennel and leeks. If I were to approach him and tell him the company wants to plant violets and nothing else, I know that will satisfy the public. We'll need to erect a couple of sheds and of course a rock wall with a locked gate to make certain the integrity of the plants remains constant."

She reached in her bag and pulled out an eight-by-ten framed picture that she handed to him. "This is Remy and his mother Rosaline when he was seventeen. Those white violets were his pride and joy in the past. Today he's developed a new strain that no one else in the world has, and no one will. He calls it the Reine Fleury after his mother.

"It grows in sun and light shade. As we say in the perfume world, it's a good doer. The blooms are prolific. In May, you can pick a bunch for the house every week until September. One of these flowers alone will fill a room with its fragrance. When the perfume comes out, it will be Ferrier's new weapon."

She'd already used it on Luc. He swallowed hard. No matter the defenses he was trying to put up, this woman was getting to him, breaking them down so fast he was growing alarmed. Luc would have to stand on his head to get the board to back this loan. Even employing his son's technology, Remy Ferrier himself was a question mark with baggage a mile long.

"Who's the Realtor?"

"Charles Boileau at the Agence Alpes-Maritime. Does his name mean anything to you?"

He handed her back the picture. "My grandfather had several dealings with him. By now he would be getting on in years."

Her eyes searched his. "What aren't you telling me?"

"As I recall, he mentioned the word crusty, but then so was my grandfather."

An unexpected laugh escaped her lips, delighting him. "What do you think would be the best way to approach him?"

Luc could feel the urgency in her. Between her passion for the project and Remy himself, plus the fact that she *had* created a new scent that could put Ferriers at the top of perfume sales, he could feel himself weakening.

"Tell you what. I'll call the agency right now. As soon as he's available, we'll go see him together, today if possible. *You* have a singular effect on everyone you meet so I want you with me. If he and the owner are agreeable to a sale and give you a price I can work with, then I'll consider taking it to my board of directors."

"Wait—" she cautioned as he reached for the cell phone in his pocket. "There are two things you need to know first."

What now? More revelations she'd been holding back? Maxim Ferrier's granddaughter was so full of them, she had him spinning. "Go ahead."

She bit the underside of her lip. He'd love a

bite of her himself and despised his weakness. "I'm not the official CEO yet."

A grimace marred his features. "Then what was that announcement about on Friday?"

"Papa left instructions that I was to be given a month before I was installed to take over the reins. He realized I'd need that long to put everything into play. But he wanted the announcement to the public made immediately to make it more difficult for the family to counteract his move."

Ciel! "If you're not the legal head yet, I can't go to the board with this. Why didn't you tell me the truth when you first came to see me?"

She stood fast. "After our precarious beginning, I didn't think I'd be able to get anywhere with you if you knew."

Luc decided he was all kinds of a fool to be taken in by her.

"I have no doubt you'll soon be hearing from some of the family on the Ferrier board, as well as Giles, claiming a show of no faith in me. If

I know them, they're already getting ready to vote me down at the next meeting a week from Friday. By preventing my installation, they'll promote the ascendancy of one of them."

No doubt. "What else haven't you told me? Don't hold anything back now," his voice rasped.

Her hesitation spoke volumes about what was coming. "Remy knows nothing about my plan yet."

Luc was incredulous. "What are you saying?"

"Exactly that."

When it registered, he said, "You mean you've had no contact with him?"

"None. I've never met him and I don't even know if he'll let me talk to him. But once I'm armed with that loan, I'll find a way." Out of dark fringed lashes, the blue burned hot with determination.

The shock of those words blocked the air he couldn't take in or out.

"I realize I should have told you all this before you offered to meet me here."

Luc took a fortifying breath. Yes, she should have told him everything, but it was also true he'd offered. With her charismatic powers of persuasion, he'd been her willing victim. She'd had those invisible hooks into him before he'd known what was happening.

"But I was afraid if I did…" Anxiety was written all over her expression, bringing out a protective instinct at odds with his frustration. "I was afraid you'd turn me down flat. This is so important. Not only is the company's life at stake, but Remy's."

The woman standing before him was a mystifying combination of warrior strength and feminine softness meant to disarm a man down to his stronghold. She'd done it to him as no other woman had done since the plane crash.

"After what I've told you about his life, can't you see that when I approach Remy and ask him to take over the company, all the negotiations have to be wrapped up behind the scenes? With the remarkable gifts he'll bring back to the company, he has to believe *I* believe in him and what he's doing."

The unspoken plea coming from her eyes would be Luc's downfall if he remained trapped by them.

Her rounded chin lifted. He sensed she'd gone into battle mode. "Because of Papa's decision, my words will ensure that the Ferrier board at least listens to me where Remy is concerned.

"But the greater weight will come from knowing it's Remy I've chosen to run the company because *he's* the rightful head who should have taken over the moment his father died. *He's* the one who can fix the company. Deep down, every staff and family member knows this, even if they won't want to admit it. I'm counting on enough of them doing the honorable thing and supporting me."

She'd left Luc nonplussed.

"If you want to tell me to go to hell right now, I won't blame you because you have every right. I certainly understand if you believe I have no conscience to get you here without your knowing all the facts. The truth is I *do* have a conscience, but this is a matter of righting a wrong, and I'm willing to do whatever it takes. Even not being totally honest with you until now."

True, she hadn't been straight with him up front. On the other hand, he'd never met a more wonderful, principled person. Without meeting Remy Ferrier, she was willing to go to these lengths for her grandfather because of the great injustice done his cousin. She wanted nothing in return for herself.

It was a heart-wrenching story, one that had a stranglehold on Luc. He'd been thinking about Remy and the tragedy that had prevented him from doing the work he'd obviously enjoyed. Even without meeting him, Luc had developed a soft spot for him, all due to Jasmine's powers of persuasion. His emotions were overwhelming him.

While he was deep in thought, she started searching in her bag. Out came her checkbook. "Since I've already committed my sin of omission with you, I'll pay you now for your time, the lunch and the mileage for your two trips to Grasse and bid you *adieu* with my heartfelt thanks."

Adieu had several meanings, one of which was "goodbye forever."

She'd just pressed the wrong button. Since the plane crash, Luc had been living cautiously in all the areas of his life. But this woman had gotten under his skin to the inner core. He didn't like the impotent way it made him feel.

A rare burst of temper welled up inside him. Forcing himself to get it under control, he said, "Why don't you put that away. The only sin you've committed is jumping to a conclusion about me."

"No—" She gave what sounded like a mournful cry. "Not over you personally, Luc. Any banker with your responsibilities and reputation would be having serious reservations after the history I've laid out for you. To plead my case with your board when I'm not legally the head of the company yet would mean you'd be doing something dishonest.

"I can't ask that of you. It's too big to expect of anyone, but I had to try. The next banker I approach will be presented the whole truth first. Please forgive me."

She tried to hand him the check she'd written, but he refused to take it. "Our clash on Yeronisos caused us to get off on the wrong foot. Before we write off this experience, let's see what kind of success we have with Monsieur Boileau. Obviously your whole plan hinges on obtaining this property to convince Remy that your papa meant business."

Without hesitation, he pressed the number to get the information operator on the line.

CHAPTER FIVE

JASMINE PUT THE check back in her purse, almost in shock that Luc was still willing to work with her after her dishonesty. Not many men would have handled the time-fused grenades she'd thrown at him with such calm; it filled her with wonder. She waited with a pounding heart while he made the vital phone call. His back was turned so she couldn't hear what he was saying.

As he shifted his weight during the conversation, she couldn't help but stare at the way his muscles moved beneath his shirt. When he suddenly turned around, she was caught studying him and there was no getting out of it with grace. Men did it to her all the time. The only thing to do was get past the moment.

"Did you reach Monsieur Boileau? What's the verdict?"

His black eyes gleamed between narrowed lids. She stifled a moan because her legs were trembling. "I was about to ask you the same question."

Hadn't she thought there was something of a bad boy about him the minute she'd seen him on Yeronisos? For the second time since she'd met him, visible heat swept over her. *You fool, Jasmine.*

"I was trying to figure out how I would have saved your unconscious body if you'd been dashed against the cliff of Yeronisos trying to outswim a great white."

One side of his mouth lifted in a devastating smile. "That's an intriguing thought. Any ideas?"

Breathe. "Not yet."

"While your scientific mind comes up with an answer, we have a date in his office at one-thirty. That ought to give us enough time to stop for lunch. I don't know about you, but I'm starving," he said in a husky voice.

She let the comment about his hunger pass. In

the last few seconds, she'd realized Luc could be a terrible tease. He swallowed her with those black eyes. "Monsieur Boileau saw you on television the other night. The man couldn't accommodate our request fast enough."

"That was nice of him."

Luc threw his head back and laughed. The rich male kind you felt invade your insides. "Do you want to follow me?"

"Since you're the hungry one, I think that's probably the wisest idea. When Dad gets hungry, he finds the shortest distance between two points. Wherever he is and *food*. I'll try to keep up with you."

More laughter ensued as they got in their cars and headed down the hillside to town. Jasmine felt so alive, she hurt with a strange kind of pain pleasure. On one of the little side streets, they found parking spaces and walked two blocks to the Gros Moine. She learned he'd eaten lunch there many times too.

A waiter seated them outside, where they enjoyed grilled swordfish and salad. "Wine?" Luc asked her.

"No, thank you. Not while I'm working." *Not while I'm with you.*

His lips twitched. "You call this work?"

She stabbed her fork into the fish. "Anything I have to do that forces me to keep my wits rules out alcohol."

He flashed her a devilish smile. "I'll remember that."

While she was attempting to recover from his remark that suggested there would be other times, the owner, who was in his fifties, came outside and headed for their table. "*La belle* Jasmine—it's always an honor to serve you."

"*Merci*, Jules. The fish is excellent as usual."

His brown eyes darted to Luc. "Is he the secret you wouldn't reveal the other night?"

"I am," sounded the deep voice she'd heard in the background of her disturbing dreams.

Luc— Her gaze flicked to him in astonishment.

Jules put a hand over his heart. "Ah...*l'amour,*

l'amour. Your secret is safe with me." He looked from her to Luc. "The waiter will bring you a complimentary dessert. Our signature *gâteau aux framboises.* Enjoy!"

The minute he walked off, she said, "You were even more audacious than Michel Didier during the interview."

He scrutinized her over the rim of his wine-glass. "I couldn't resist. Jules has a crush on you as bad as the TV anchorman's. So does my as-sistant, Thomas. Monsieur Boileau is already salivating in anticipation of your arrival."

She smiled as she shook her head. "I have to admit, you're good at talking the talk, Lucien Charriere." With the exception of that time on the island when she'd thought he was trying to pick her up, it was better than any talk she'd ever heard from another Frenchman. It was be-cause when he spoke, it didn't sound like a line.

One black brow lifted dangerously. "Then I've passed your test?"

"Which one is that?"

All the amusement left his eyes. "The only one that counts."

If she spent much more time with him, she would need to visit a cardiologist. "If I were to meet your mother, I suspect she'd tell me you were a handful the moment you could stand up in your crib."

"Much more than that," he quipped. "My parents are away on a trip at the moment. When they return, you can ask her. I'll make a point of it."

The waiter didn't deliver their raspberry tart a moment too soon. She took several bites. In France you didn't bring a woman home to meet your mother unless you'd been brought to your knees. She could hardly breathe.

"What size family do you have?"

"An older sister and brother, both married with children. My extended family is large. We have aunts, uncles and cousins everywhere in the vicinity. I'll answer your next question now. My father heads a multinational financial services corporation specializing in retail brokerage."

"Why aren't you working with him?"

"The stock market involves too much risk. I prefer not to head into old age with ulcers. My grandfather enjoyed a less frenetic existence in the banking world and lived to a ripe old age."

More guilt attacked her for asking so much of him. She rested her fork on the plate. "I've put you between a rock and a hard place, haven't I?"

He finished off his tart. "I always enjoyed *The Man in the Iron Mask*. For once in my life, it might be challenging to help the side of a nobler cause and put the rightful king on the throne. The idea of it appeals to a part of my deeply buried instinct for adventure."

Jasmine was intrigued by the admission. Something of significance lay behind it. "Why deeply buried?"

"One of these days, I might tell you." That sounded cryptic. "If you've finished, shall we go?" He put some bills on the table. "The Realtor's office is on the other side of Grasse. I'm eager to watch you work the magic that went out over the airwaves on Friday evening to mesmerize your fascinated audience."

He helped her up from the table and they left for their cars. She got in behind the wheel and looked at him through the open window. "Working with my papa *was* magical. But the whole time I was talking, I feared Remy and his family might be watching. Then again, he probably made sure he didn't see any of it to block out the horrendously painful memories."

Luc pressed his forehead against the top of the door, bringing their faces closer together. "I'd like to be the proverbial fly on the wall when you present your case to him. Your concern for him broke my heart, Jasmine. If he's the man you say he is, then your words will transform him."

Her throat almost closed. "I pray they do," she whispered.

She had the impression he wanted to kiss her. Or maybe it was because she wanted him to. While she waited for it with an ache that wouldn't go away, he turned and strode swiftly toward his car, devastating her. Appalled and frightened by these new emotions pouring out of her, she rummaged shakily for her keys and started the engine.

When she'd started out from the house this morning, she'd hoped Luc would give her a chance once he'd seen the property. Now that he was doing his part on blind faith, to want anything more from him embarrassed her. She'd actually sat there waiting to feel his mouth close over hers!

"I'll be right behind you," she called to him. Her heart raced as she tried to keep up with him. He drove fast before finding the building in question, where they each found a parking spot. The prosperous agency listed a dozen agents with Monsieur Boileau's name being at the top.

Luc entered the reception area with Jasmine. The receptionist soon led them down the hall to his office. The sixtyish, balding Realtor was all smiles as he got up from his chair and hurried toward them. Luc introduced her.

"It's a real honor to meet the new chief at Ferriers, Ms. Martin."

"Thank you for meeting with us so quickly."

"Monsieur Charriere indicated your business borders on an emergency."

She owed Luc everything and darted him a quiet smile. "He's right. There's a time element involved."

"Then let's all sit down and you tell me what I can do for you."

Luc sat back in his chair and handed the file to her. It was clear he was leaving this up to her. In that regard, he reminded her of her papa, who had seen her as an equal and never talked over her head. She appreciated that more than he could know.

"I'm aware it hasn't been advertised, but I understand the old abbey property is for sale again. I would like to buy it for the company."
Jasmine spent the next few minutes explaining what she wanted it for and how it would be de-

veloped. She handed him some papers from the file. "The owner couldn't object to the projected use of the land. With this sale, everyone would be handsomely compensated and preserve the tradition of the fields."

His bushy eyebrows knit together. "I'm sorry to say that someone else has already put in a bid for it."

"I was afraid of that."

"Do you have an earnest money agreement?" Luc questioned.

A ruddy color entered the older man's cheeks. He cleared his throat. "I'm not at liberty to tell you that."

"A verbal bid isn't solid, which means you don't have one yet," Luc came back with startling authority. The Realtor didn't really have a buyer and Luc had known it at the outset. It was all a bluff to see how much money the agency could wangle out of Ferriers, but Luc wouldn't let him get away with it. "What's your asking price?"

Monsieur Boileau named an eight-digit figure

that was higher than she'd anticipated, causing her spirits to plummet.

"No wonder you don't have a sale yet. If your other client exists, which I doubt, then I presume they're in the process of finding the backing needed. But knowing the market as I do, you're not going to get that price from anyone," Luc rapped out.

His remarks had unsettled the older man.

"Lower it by two million euros and Ms. Martin might be interested. You have it in writing that Ferriers will treat the land the way it was meant to be used. That will satisfy the seller. Otherwise it will sit there for another twenty years, and you know it."

The other man sat there touching his fingertips together while he considered the offer. Jasmine was afraid to make a move. Luc had taken over with a fearsome mastery that proved why he'd been made director of the bank at such a young age. In action, he was awesome. His shrewd business skills had read the situation accurately.

Another minute and the man sat forward. "You're ready to sign now?" She could see the dollar signs in his eyes. That meant Luc had gotten to him.

"If you'd give me and my client a minute to confer, we'd appreciate it."

"Of course."

He got up from his desk and left the room. After he'd shut the door Jasmine turned to Luc in panic. "You haven't presented anything to your banking board yet. I thought you told me it would be too risky as long as I wasn't the official CEO yet."

"I have more information to work with than I had when you first approached me. Here's what needs to happen, Jasmine. I'll be happy to authorize your signing an earnest money agreement today with the Realtor, provided you approach Remy Ferrier right away. He needs to be in agreement with your plan, and then he needs to meet with me. If all goes well, then I'll grant the loan and you can come back here to buy the property."

"But I don't want you to jeopardize your position at the bank! Naturally I'm overjoyed at what is happening, but not at the cost of you doing something you could regret."

"Don't let that be your concern right now. As far as I'm concerned, it's Remy Ferrier you need to worry about. You can show him the signed earnest money agreement offer. It should be the proof he needs to know you're behind him a thousand percent. I'll take care of the rest."

She shot out of the chair. "But not if it isn't aboveboard. I won't let you do something that harms you!"

"It won't. To be honest, you've convinced me the man's life is at stake, along with a company that should have been his. If there's risk involved, I find myself wanting to take it for the sake of an ideal."

There couldn't be another man in the world like Luc, but she couldn't possibly let him do it. "Don't think I don't appreciate what you're trying to do here, but we're going to leave. On the way out, I'll tell the Realtor I've changed my mind."

Luc barred her path. "What were Carton's last words in *A Tale of Two Cities*? 'It's a far, far better thing that I do, than I have ever done.'" His eyes burned like coals. "You've taught me that, Jasmine. Monsieur Boileau is ready to do business, so do it!"

There were dimensions to this man she couldn't have known were there when they'd first met. Was it only several months ago?

"But, Luc—what if Remy won't be able to accept what his cousin wanted to do for him?"

He eyed her with singular intent. "Then you'll lose the money on the earnest agreement, that's all. However, I believe in you to get the job done."

"But what if I'm wrong and Remy can't save the company? Then everything you've done will have been in vain."

He shook his dark head. "You do have a backup plan, *n'est-ce pas*?"

She took a shuddering breath. "Of course.

I'll find a buyer for the property and pay you back with triple interest. If I can't accomplish that in a reasonable period of time, I'll deed La Tourette over to you."

Her papa had already willed the house and property to her. She in turn planned to will everything back to Remy as planned. But if he refused what was rightfully his, and she couldn't find a buyer, then she would make certain it went to Luc.

"You see?" he inserted. "None of this will have been in vain. One step at a time, Jasmine. Shall I tell him to come back in?"

She lifted her eyes to him. "Are you sure about this?"

He moved closer and squeezed her arm. She felt its warmth seep in. "I've never been so sure of anything in my life."

His belief in her ability to carry this off rated even higher than her papa's belief in her, if that was possible. Luc wasn't family. Less than two weeks ago they had been strangers except for the incident on Yeronisos island. She couldn't pretend to understand his true motive for getting involved like this. But she wasn't so naïve that she didn't know he would demand something of her in return.

However one fact was clear. He *did* trust her. What greater gift had anyone ever given her? While she was still trying to comprehend it, the Realtor tapped on the door and poked his head in. "Do you need more time?"

His voice jerked her back to the present. She turned to him. "No. I'm ready to put down earnest money with a time frame of one week." Jasmine had to track down Remy and that might prove difficult.

The older man rubbed his hands together. She'd anticipated that reaction. Within twenty minutes the transaction was complete with funds out of the account her papa had set up for her. More handshakes ensued before Luc walked her out to her car.

"What are you going to do with the rest of this day, as if I didn't know?" he asked after she'd climbed in.

She put the file of papers aside and glanced up at him. "You mean this red-letter day that wouldn't have been possible without you? While I'm still full of endorphins from your selfless gift, I'm going to figure out the best way to meet Remy. I have to approach him at the right time."

"It was anything but selfless."

Jasmine had to take another quick breath. His real reasons for deciding to help her were still unexplained, but she'd find them out later. "Whatever motivated you, I'm in your debt."

"I only ask one favor." *Here it comes.* She braced herself. "Whatever the result of your meeting with Remy, call me when you've had your talk with him."

That favor was far too easy to grant. The blood pounded in her ears. "You'll be the first person to know everything, but I have no idea how soon I'll be getting in touch with you. I don't know how soon Remy will be available."

"True, but a flower farmer isn't long parted from his crop."

He understood a lot. "You're right."

Luc backed away from the door. "You know where to find me."

In the next breath, she glimpsed an unexpected look of triumph in the recesses of his eyes. For an inexplicable reason, her body underwent a curious shiver. Reaction was already settling in over the enormity of what she'd just allowed to happen.

"À bientôt," he called over his shoulder before heading for his Jaguar, leaving her with an ache as she drove home to La Tourette.

On Thursday morning, Jasmine headed for the old, small Fleury farmhouse on the outskirts of Grasse. She owed Luc for helping her get this far, even if she didn't know at what cost yet. Because of him, she was able to put her plan into action much sooner than she'd thought.

Now it was up to her to make it all bear fruit for this seminal moment in two lives. But so much was against her, she trembled with fear.

When Jasmine looked at herself in the mirror,

she had a hard time seeing anyone but herself. Those around her who knew her father saw his dark blue eyes and nose in her. Those who knew her grandfather saw his rich dark hair and the shape of his brows in her. Those who knew her mother saw the pure oval of her face.

But the majority of her world saw the overlay of her grandmother Megan in Jasmine's countenance, from the outline of her smile, to the rare frown on her forehead, to the occasional wistful expression, to the shape of her figure.

That's what frightened Jasmine. Two cousins had loved her grandmother with a wild passion that would go on through eternity. Megan had loved them both. But though Remy had found her first, it was to Jasmine's grandfather she'd given her heart.

When Remy looked at Jasmine, would he be able to get past the reminder of her grandmother long enough to listen to what she had to say? Did the pain still pierce so deeply, he wouldn't be able to bear it?

Her entire body trembled as she drove along the modest piece of ground laid out in rows of violets on her way to reach the house. She slowed down when she saw a man hunkered down tending one of the plants under the morning sun. He wore denims and a white shirt with the sleeves shoved up to the elbows. His back was to her.

Even from the distance she recognized the burnished red hair and was reminded of Luc's comment about a farmer and his crop. Being sixty-six hadn't faded the color or changed the strong physique that could have belonged to a much younger man. Jasmine had thought him very handsome in all the pictures.

He hadn't seen her yet. She pulled the car to a stop.

This was it.

Putting the file in her straw bag, she got out of the front seat and stepped over the ridge of ground to reach the *terroir*. The heavenly scent was close to overpowering. She got to within a couple of yards of him.

"Eh bien." She cleared her throat. "I'm looking for Remy Fleury Ferrier."

He jumped to his feet and turned around. For a timeless moment he looked at her until his green eyes began to burn and he staggered backwards. She knew the woman he was seeing. No doubt he had watched Jasmine's broadcast. Even deeply tanned, she could tell he'd paled.

"Mon Dieu," he whispered as if he'd seen a ghost.

"You and I don't share the same blood, but I share a love of this land you love to the marrow of your bones. You're the son who should have been put in as the head of the Ferrier empire the second your father died."

Emotion darkened the green of his eyes.

"I'm Jasmine, a nose of little consequence. My grandfather used me so I could get you installed to your rightful place as CEO of a company that you built years ago. It needs you desperately."

Taking advantage of his speechless state, Jasmine reached in her bag and handed him the file. "Read this and you'll see that the Banque Internationale du Midi is loaning us the money to buy the old abbey property. The CEO, Lucien Charriere, wants to meet you. Here's the record of the earnest money agreement. If you're willing to take over the company, then this land will be ours and we're going to plant thousands more of your fabulous Parma violets.

"I've already made up the perfume from the ones I bought at the flower market on Saturday.

"Here's a sample." She pressed the little bottle into his other hand. "I think we should call it Parfum Reine Fleury, after your mother.

"With you at the helm, the company will come back so much greater than it's been. Unfortunately life dealt the family a monstrous blow under the rule of your despotic father. Forgive me for being so brutal, but not all men who can make a baby are fit for husbandom or fatherdom."

She took a step closer. "I've heard about you all my life. Except for the ability to get inside your skin, I know the long, twisted, painful history that drove you away. Papa loved you so much and told me everything."

A strange sound, suspiciously like a sob, escaped his throat.

She pulled out the picture. "This is my favorite photo of you that your mother put up on the stairway. The stairway of *your* house, Remy. Here's the deed made out to you. You're the legal owner of the house and the property. No one else." She handed it to him. He took it. By now, his arms and hands were loaded. He moved as if he were in a dream.

"I feel a bit like King Richard who knighted Robin Hood and said, 'All former residences and manors are restored to you.' What do you say to that, Sir Robin of Loxley?"

His throat was working. She could feel the emotions erupting inside him.

"Will you let me hug you, dear Remy? I've loved you for so long and have been waiting for this moment for what seems like an eternity. Please," she begged in an aching voice.

After a stillness that almost destroyed her, he

put the things down, then extended his arms. She ran into them and they hugged while unspoken messages passed between them. His body quietly heaved.

Tears rolled down her cheeks. "Papa cried to me over you more times than you can possibly imagine. His plan was to put me in charge until I could convince you to come back home where you always belonged." She eased away, but still held on to his arms, which she shook.

"You have to believe that. Papa went to the other side early, but I know he'll never rest in peace until you accept his love and forgive him. Don't you know in your soul he loved you? He said your name on his dying breath."

Remy expelled a great, shuddering sigh. "I loved Max too. He didn't do anything wrong. My father was the one responsible for hurting my mother and me. But in my anger I blamed Max for everything. It took me years to come to grips with the truth about my life, about Megan. She and Max had always been honest with me, but I chose to believe they betrayed me.

"When I married Louise and we had a baby, my feelings started to undergo a change. But my wife was too upset about never having enough money and left me and Jean-Louis. The truth is *he* became my salvation.

"After he got older and married, I talked to him frankly about my life. That's when I decided to go to Max and beg *his* forgiveness for the way I treated him." Tears filled his eyes. "But he died unexpectedly."

"It was a shock to all of us."

"I wrote a letter to Megan telling her what was in my heart. She wrote me back, telling me that my letter had released her from pain. I suffered another shock when I heard about her death so soon after."

"Oh, Remy." She hugged him again. "Don't suffer anymore. I'm sure they both now know how you feel and are content. The only thing left is for you to take over the company."

He smiled. "Except for one thing. I don't believe the family is going to throw their arms around an ancient, formerly bitter, recovered alcoholic as you have done."

"You're not ancient, and they aren't your blood. *You're* the true Ferrier, and they will thrill to the knowledge that you're going to save everyone's skins because there isn't anyone else! Give them a chance. There are years of life ahead! You *are* going to accept!"

A chuckle escaped his throat. "Do I have a choice?"

"None!"

"Come to the house and meet the family."

"I'm dying to." He picked up the things. She linked her arm through his and they started walking. "Any noses born yet?"

He actually laughed through the tears. Except for Luc's, it was the most beautiful sound she'd ever heard.

Friday morning, Luc's cell phone rang. After two hellish nights with no sleep, he sprang out of bed and grabbed the phone off the nightstand. At last! The one name he'd wanted to see on the caller ID had finally appeared.

He clicked on. "Jasmine?"

"Forgive me for calling you this early, Luc, but I wanted to catch you before you left for work. I need your advice. Would you have time for a quick breakfast first? I'll meet you at Chez Arnaud near your bank. It'll be my treat."

Since they'd parted company the day before yesterday, the torturous wait to hear from her had driven him up a wall. Luc's pulse raced. "How soon can you get here?" He would have told her he'd meet her anywhere, but since she already had a plan in mind, so much the better.

"Half an hour."

"I'll be there."

"My debt to you keeps growing." On that note, she clicked off.

Those endorphins she'd talked about filled his system. Today wasn't going to be the day without her in it he'd been dreading. He showered and shaved in record time. Reaching for one of his suits, he dressed for work. Already he had plans for the end of the day that would include Jasmine. She just didn't know it yet.

His breathing altered when he arrived and saw her seated at one of the small round tables outside, dressed in another blouse and skirt like she'd worn yesterday. She was ready for work. If there was any difference in her, it was the full smile she bestowed on him. It illuminated his insides. Jasmine had good news or her eyes wouldn't be shining a bluer blue than the sea beyond them.

"Thanks for meeting me on such short notice, Luc. I took the liberty of ordering breakfast for both of us so you wouldn't be held up."

"I appreciate that." He sat down opposite her. "Right now I want to hear about Remy. You caught up with him obviously."

After the waiter served their breakfast and poured coffee, she said, "Yesterday morning, I found him on his farm tending the violets. It proved, among other things, that you're clair-voyant."

"This is the land of flowers. You can't drive

by a field without someone in it. Now tell me what it was like to meet him."

Her eyes filled, but the tears stayed on her dark lashes. "Oh, Luc—he's so wonderful!"

Jasmine's compassion for another human being's pain had stirred Luc's deepest emotions. "How long are you going to keep me in suspense?"

She laughed gently. "For the first five minutes, I did all the talking. I thought he'd never respond. At the height of my agony, he held out his arms." Her shoulders started to shake. She was trying to hold back her emotions in front of him.

"It's strange, but he feels so familiar to me, like he's my long lost great uncle. Our talk was cathartic. I love him, and I know he's more than up to the job of running the company. You'll think so too after talking to him."

That was the moment when Luc recognized something earthshaking had happened to him and there wasn't anything he could do about it.

"We spent the rest of the day and last night

discussing everything," she went on talking. "He's willing to take on the company, but he knows it will be an uphill battle to win a majority vote. I told him you want to meet him since you're the person he'll be doing bank business with in the future. How soon do you want him to come to your office?"

Luc had to think fast. Thomas could clear part of today's schedule. "This afternoon? Two o'clock?"

"That's perfect! He'll be there." Her eyes glistened. "One more thing I'd like to ask of you if you don't mind. I need your advice about something else only you can help me with."

He didn't know how much more of this he could take. "What would that be?"

"When your grandfather put your name up to be considered to take his place, how did he do it when there were other men older than you with experience who wanted the position? Did he meet privately with each member of the board?"

Luc was so blindsided by the realization that he was madly, painfully in love with Jasmine

Ferrier, he hardly heard her questions. He'd known love's power in his late teens, but tragedy had struck, turning him into a different man, who'd been closed up ever since.

No longer a teenager, he was a grown man of thirty-four who'd possibly lived half his life already. But a big portion of that life had been half lived to avoid future pain of loss. In scientific terms, it meant he'd lived to a point when life had fallen to half its value and the other half would grow unstable. That was the path he'd been on.

"Luc?" The sound of Jasmine's concerned voice jerked him back to the present. "Are you all right?"

He fought to recover. Her request for his advice had humbled him, but he worried. Once she didn't need him anymore, would she want him as much as he wanted her? He needed to get back to the office and think.

"Forgive me, Jasmine. I want to answer your questions, but not here while we're both still facing a full work day ahead of us. On my way over here, my assistant alerted me to a problem I need to take care of before my first appointment. I'm sorry, but I have to go."

He finished his roll and drank some coffee. "Why don't I call you after my meeting with Remy and we'll talk then." He got up from the table.

"Of course," she said in a quiet voice. "Thank you for agreeing to meet me at all, Luc."

Their eyes met. "I told you to let me know after you'd seen Remy. I'm looking forward to meeting him. Talk to you later." He put some bills on the table and walked off. Though he thought he heard her call to him, he kept on going.

When Remy Ferrier arrived at his office at two that afternoon and sat down with him, Luc couldn't have been more surprised over the man's dynamic aura. He felt as if he were talking to a man in his fifties! Maxim Ferrier's cousin was every bit as charming, sophisticated and intelligent, but in an entirely different way.

They talked at length about the new technology his son had developed. After discussing some of Remy's marketing ideas for the future of flower farming, Luc realized this extraordinary man had vision and depth of character. Ferriers couldn't possibly go wrong with him at the helm.

"If the board can't see their way to voting me in, then so be it. For Jasmine to come to me on behalf of my cousin has meant everything. She has touched my life and I'll always be grateful. Thank you for all you've done."

"It's been my pleasure." Luc could hear Jasmine's defense that Remy was wonderful. She was right. He was a wonderful person. He talked about his love for his cousin, who'd tried everything on earth to get him to come back and head the company after Paul died. But he couldn't do it then.

Before Remy left the office, he said, "I know none of this would be possible if you hadn't listened to Jasmine. She has a lot of her grandmother Megan in her. Yesterday when she came to the farm and begged me to take over the family business, it was like being with Megan again." His voice sounded husky. "There's a sweetness and earnestness in her. I found I couldn't say no. I couldn't love her more if she were my own granddaughter."

Remy had revealed a world of information with that admission. Luc had known there was an underlying problem that had kept Remy away. That problem had been a woman, Maxim Ferrier's wife. In the end, Remy hadn't been able to say no to Jasmine either. Luc didn't know the story. One day, he'd get Jasmine to tell him.

Once Remy left the bank, Luc phoned the woman who was continually in his thoughts. She answered on the second ring. Besides being anxious to hear about Remy, he hoped she'd been just as eager to hear Luc's voice. She had his insides so twisted up, he didn't know himself anymore.

"In a word, Remy is the man for the job in every way. I have no doubt of it. Why don't you and I take a drive to the top of the gorge this evening? There's a quaint inn that serves lamb wrapped in mint leaves and roasted over a wood fire."

"I haven't been there in years, but I remember it was delicious."

"Good. It will give us all the privacy and time we need to talk strategy."

She took her time before she said, "I probably won't be through with work before six."

"Fine. Let's say seven at your house. I'd rather pick you up there than at your lab. That way we suffer less chance of being seen together before you drop another bomb in your family's lap. I'm looking forward to our meeting tonight." That was the understatement of all time.

He clicked off and went in his house to get ready. After a shower and shave, he put on an open-necked sport shirt and trousers. The talk with Nic earlier in the week had helped him get his feelings out in the open. As his friend had said, move past all the business first. That's what Luc intended to do so they could get down to the personal. He needed to be with her tonight.

When he left the house, he decided to keep the top down. The scent of the flowers rising from the farms in the warm evening air affected him like an aphrodisiac.

Luc knew where to go. He'd been to the Ferrier home many years ago with his grandfather on business. He'd sat outside in the sedan while he'd waited for him. With the cypress and orange trees lining the gravel drive, the setting was the envy of everyone who visited the perfume fields of the Midi.

Little had he known that a certain young granddaughter had been a frequent visitor quietly following in Maxim Ferrier's footsteps. Maybe she'd even been there at the same time as Luc. His heart thundered in his chest anticipating being with her tonight. He had no intention of ever letting her get away from him. To make sure of it, he'd pulled out every stop to ensure there could be no escape route.

As he drew up in front of the house, she

appeared wearing a filmy, soft orange-colored dress. He'd come early and there she was. The skirt draped around her long, elegant legs with every step. She'd caught her hair back with a clip. Luc's breath caught at the mold of her enticing figure.

Their eyes met as he got out of the car and walked around to help her in. "You're wearing a different perfume this evening."

"I didn't put on any. It must be the shampoo."

"You smell like fresh peaches."

She darted him a glance after he'd started the engine. "I hope you like them. Papa developed the scent. For a non-nose, you have a keen olfactory sense. Maybe you're in the wrong business."

Luc chuckled. "Before we leave, shall I put the top up?"

"Please don't. I love the breeze. You can smell everything growing."

"That's why I bought a convertible."

She smiled. "I'm surprised everyone doesn't drive one here. For years I've worked in a shadowy lab. It's a treat to be in the open air and breathe all the scents. When I'm home, I live outside."

Her comment threw him. His head jerked around. "You *are* home."

"No. You could say Grasse has been my second home because of my grandparents. But my home is in Driggs, Idaho, where I help on the ranch. There's nothing I love more than riding my horse through the sage. When it has just rained, the scent is so heavy, it's almost as overpowering as the jasmine in flower. I miss it. As soon as Remy takes over, I'll be leaving."

"You mean on a well-earned vacation."

"No. I mean for good. I'm afraid I'm like Papa. I don't want to be the head of anything. That's why I'm so grateful you've helped me get everything into place this fast."

His hands gripped the steering wheel with so much force, he had to slow down before they had an accident. Suddenly his world was blowing up in his face. "I don't understand. Your papa designated you to be the nose for the company. All the years you've put in…"

"Luc, I had to get my degree in something and will never regret any of the time I spent with him. But now that I've secretly created a violet perfume from the violets Remy has been growing, I have other interests and have worked it out with him."

"Worked out *what* exactly?" he demanded. His adrenaline had kicked in.

"When he wants to put another new product on the market, he'll use the other chemists in the lab. If they run into a problem, he'll call me and I'll fly over to help."

His mind was reeling. In his gut, he sensed there was only one reason Jasmine planned to go back to the States.

A man.

But she was keeping it a secret until she'd carried out her agenda here to install Remy. That's why she'd avoided the question the anchorman had asked about someone special in her life.

Was he a rancher like her father? Had she

already committed to him? She wore no ring, but that didn't mean anything if she was in love with him.

If that was the case, why hadn't he been with her in Cyprus?

Luc was riddled with questions, particularly since he'd felt the sensual tension growing between them from the moment they'd met. He couldn't have been wrong about that. It was so real he didn't recognize the man he'd become since their meeting on Yeronisos.

Before tonight was over, he intended to find out the truth. Hearing about her plan to fly away forever gave him a feeling that wasn't any different from being in the plane after it lost power. When he'd seen the earth coming up to meet him, his world had flashed before his eyes then too. But he wasn't about to relive that aftermath a second time.

CHAPTER SIX

NIP IT IN the bud. That's what you did when you didn't want the plant to grow bigger.

Judging by the quiet coming from Luc, she'd accomplished her objective. But that didn't help her state of mind. Far from it.

Remy had told Jasmine about his son's new scientific discovery, called a bio-timer mechanism. It helped synchronize growth and control the rate. This would allow the farmer to save on man power and shipping because maturing crops wouldn't all flower at the same time. It could save Ferriers hundreds of thousands of dollars.

"We'll maximize our yield and reduce the cost of harvesting because you can do it all at once and reduce waste."

The phenomenal discovery was another

weapon in Remy's arsenal, but she'd just applied it to the situation with Luc Charriere.

Jasmine was already in deeper than she wanted to be with him. Once she'd picked his brains tonight, she didn't plan on seeing him again. Being up-front with him right now about where her life was going was its own control mechanism.

By making it clear that her meetings with him had been for business only, she would stop the growth of something that couldn't be. It was time to make the break. Her future was in Idaho. She'd promised this to herself and her parents, whose hearts she'd broken. Then maybe her guilt would go away.

Jasmine had been living with all kinds of remorse since her parents' last visit. The pain and disappointment in their eyes had tortured her until she couldn't live with it any longer.

When Luc reached the inn, they were shown around the side and seated in a garden. So far they were the only diners in this section, but it wouldn't be long before more arrived. A mist watering the flowers cooled the hot air around them. The delightful setting provided the perfect ambience for her business meeting with him. But with her heart in her throat, she'd never felt less businesslike in her life.

When she eyed him with a covert glance, his newly shaven jaw still retained its shadow and had taken on a chiseled, almost primitive cast. It reminded her once more of his Ligurian ancestry, those warriors who'd fought with ferocity against the Romans. The thought unnerved her no end.

A waiter took their order for the lamb. Jasmine asked for coffee. "Make that two," Luc spoke up. Then he lounged back in the chair and came straight to the point.

"To answer the question you asked me at breakfast, my grandfather knew it would be an uphill battle to get me appointed. He couldn't see that a meeting with each board member would change their prejudice. Their perception, naturally, was that I didn't have the gravitas. In the end, he called them together in one body and let me speak. Either I could make my own case with a vision of where the bank should be going, or not."

"Your grandfather knew you could pull it off," Jasmine said, studying him intently. "That's why it worked. Thank you for giving me the answer I needed. After being with Remy, I know in my bones he'll wield that same power."

Luc sat forward. "He has the necessary gravitas?"

"Yes. As for you, you were born with a unique power to get things done. I saw it in front of Monsieur Boileau. No one could have taught it to you, Luc. Remy has that same kind of power. Though he's a son of the soil, he's also a man of the world with refined sensitivity who understands people. The board is ignorant of his value, but they won't be for long.

"Instead of my trying to convince them, I'm going to take a leaf out of your grandfather's book and let him speak for himself. Once they hear him present his ideas and understand his great grasp of the company he put on the map, he'll hold them in the palm of his hand."

"I agree, Jasmine. He impressed me in surprising ways. I know he'll have that same effect on your board members."

"I'm so glad you feel that way!" she cried. "After he speaks to them, I'll remind them that the only reason there's a company today and the only reason they have a job is because of Remy. Hundreds of families who work for the company in the region still feel a deep loyalty to him and will cheer his election.

"Though Paul had a nose, it wasn't that great and he couldn't have succeeded without Papa. And before you can make up a perfume recipe and sell it, you have to have the knowledge and the infrastructure behind you. That was Remy."

She waited for Luc to say something.

"When is the meeting?" he asked at last, but she saw no warmth in those black eyes. What wasn't he telling her? Something troubling was going on inside of him.

"A week from Monday, but I'm going to move it up to a week from today."

"That's very soon."

"Exactly. The element of surprise will work in Remy's favor."

Once the waiter served them, Luc asked, "Won't it still work if you wait until the Monday already chosen? Why the great rush?"

She ate some tender morsels of lamb. "You don't know the family board members. They're festering now. The less time they have to speculate and make the situation more difficult, the better."

"And the sooner you can go home," he muttered before eating his food.

"Yes. I can't wait to get back to my family."

Jasmine averted her eyes, conflicted by her own decision to leave France and get on with a new life. All sense of family had disappeared here in France once her grandparents were buried. Since then, her guilt over spending so much time away from her parents had caught up to her. She needed to go home and make up for all the lost time.

But the striking male seated across from her could have no idea how his existence was causing her emotional upheaval that she couldn't have imagined before meeting him on the island.

He still didn't say anything and it made her nervous. "The house is Remy's. I've already started packing up my things. I told him to start moving in. Papa never allowed anyone to disturb Remy's or his mother's suite of rooms. All his treasures are still there waiting for him. His son and wife and the grandchildren will be overjoyed. They're cramped in the Fleury farmhouse."

Filled with anxiety at this point, she blurted, "But I haven't forgotten my promise to you— if the family won't vote for Remy, at least he'll have his home and land back. I'll find a buyer for the old abbey property. Fortunately I have a few sources I can contact to make certain you're paid back with interest."

"Let's not worry about that right now."

He remained quiet throughout the rest of their dinner. Feeling more and more uncomfortable, she said no to another cup of coffee. There'd be no sleep for her tonight as it was.

Finally she couldn't stand the tension any longer. "It's growing late and I've taken up enough of your time. I'm ready to leave when you are."

One black brow lifted. "Are you meeting with Remy tonight?"

"No."

"Then why the hurry?"

Heat swarmed into her face. "Because I got you up early this morning and feel guilty about it. You have a half-hour drive ahead of you tonight and a full banking day tomorrow."

"I'm a big boy now in case you didn't notice. I get up and go to bed when I please."

"Of course. I'm just so grateful for everything you've done, I'm embarrassed at how much time of yours I've taken when—when—" Rarely had she ever been at a loss for words.

"When I could be with another woman? Is that what you were going to say?"

"No," she lied.

"In other words you're not interested in my private life."

"It's none of my business." The charged atmosphere had her trembling.

"Go ahead and ask me if there's a woman in my life."

She lifted her head in torment. "Luc—"

"There've been many women over the years, but I never wanted to live with one of them, let alone get married."

Beneath the cynical sounding revelation, Jasmine thought she detected a thread of pain. "Why?"

He shook his dark head. "It's your turn. Who's the man of special interest in your life in Idaho you can't get back to soon enough? A cowboy who's waiting impatiently for your return?" he drawled.

She couldn't believe he'd just said that and

grabbed on to his assumption like a lifeline. "And if there is?"

When you didn't want to answer a question, then answer it with another one. That fictional man had to be out there somewhere! Jasmine was counting on it because she'd promised to live with her family from now on. She wanted a husband and family of her own where they could all be together.

Jasmine didn't think Luc's eyes could go any blacker, but they did. "Is he a friend of your family?" he kept it up. "A fellow rancher perhaps?"

"I'd rather we got off the subject if you don't mind."

"Why?" he persisted. "Is it too painful to talk about?"

Taking a deep breath she said, "Maybe I'll answer your question when you answer mine."

The hard line of his mouth relaxed. "So you *are* interested."

He had her there. "Only if you feel like sharing."

She could hear his mind ticking. "I fell for

a girl in high school. We were planning to get married in the fall after graduation. *Je l'aimais à la folie*." To hear him say he'd been madly in love sent a pain to her heart. "When you're young, you feel everything intensely and imagine yourself immortal. One weekend, our group of six, including my best friend, decided to go skydiving."

What Jasmine heard next tore her up inside. It was a miracle he'd survived the crash.

"I'd always been the one to suggest the more dangerous activities. But my sense of adventure overtook common sense one too many times. There was a price to be paid. One of the results was that I discovered you can't count on the permanence of life.

"Marriage was no longer part of my future agenda. But that doesn't mean to say I don't enjoy women thoroughly…as you've already discovered," he added.

She couldn't look at him for a minute. Her pain for him went too deep.

"Now it's your turn, Jasmine."

But all she could think of was the terrible pain he'd lived through. "That explains why you were so vehement about me not going cliff jumping. It makes sense now. I could tell you were more than a little upset. How horrible for you, Luc. I'm so sorry."

"It happened a long time ago. I hadn't thought about it in years until I heard a couple of the teenagers scream and I had a flashback. When I saw you start for the steps of the cliff, I was seized by fear for you. I was afraid there could be another tragedy."

"I understand and I was an idiot not to let you know I didn't plan to participate."

"Not an idiot. You had no idea who I was or what I might have been up to. Unfortunately there are enough awful things that happen to innocent people to force you to protect yourself."

She looked around, seemingly conscious of the other diners. "Why don't we talk in the car on the way home? We're not the only people out here anymore."

"You're right, and everyone is staring at you.

Whether they recognize you from television or not, you will always draw attention, just like your grandmother, Megan."

Her gaze flicked to his. "Remy must have talked to you about her."

"Only that you reminded him of her and he couldn't say no to you. Did he love her?"

"Yes," she whispered. "You figured that out?"

"It wasn't something he could hide. I doubt he was even aware of it."

"Papa always feared Remy would never get over loving her too." Jasmine looked away. "Let's go."

On the way to her house, Luc drove past the land she intended to purchase and pulled over to the side for a minute. Night had fallen over the landscape. He reflected that the soil here in Grasse was coveted by the farmers of the world for its exceptional ingredients, producing flowers of the highest quality.

But as he looked out to the sea, Luc realized Grasse possessed many more qualities not found anywhere else. With the gentle breeze blowing off the water to dishevel Jasmine's hair, the land, the twinkling lights of villas seemed locked in a kind of intangible enchantment.

Without eyeing her, he said, "Can you honestly walk away from this and leave Remy to carry the load alone?"

He heard her shallow intake of breath. "He's getting his life back and has his own family to help him. I have loved ones waiting for me at home."

Luc turned to her. "Why wasn't this special man with you on Yeronisos?"

She wouldn't look at him. He sensed her calm was forced.

"Ranching isn't unlike farming. To coin your phrase a different way, Luc, a rancher isn't long separated from his cattle herd."

"Not even for the woman he loves?" She was evading him. "Is he divorced with a child?"

She gasped. "Why on earth would you ask that?"

"It's a legitimate question. A rancher has a

foreman to take care of things if he wants to get away, but if he has a child to consider, that makes it more complicated to arrange a trip. Is that why you're turning your back on part of who you are? Has he asked you to marry him and help raise his child? To consider what you're planning to do means you would have to be driven by a compelling reason."

"For heaven's sake, Luc—"

She was sounding more and more flustered. He flicked her a glance. "I can't fathom a man who wants to marry you leaving you alone for a second. How much do you truly love him when you've been separated so much of the time?"

Her inability to come up with a response convinced him she was hiding something. He had enough patience to wait until they were in a less public spot to find out what was going on inside her. After a couple of cars drove by, he pulled back on the road and headed down the gorge.

The moment he pulled up in front of her house, he saw her hand reach for the door handle. "Careful. I haven't turned off the engine yet. Why are you acting so frightened of me?"

She took an unsteady breath. "It's not fear, Luc. I simply don't want to take up any more of your time."

"Would you still say that if there weren't a man waiting for your return?"

A sound of exasperation came out of her before she turned to him. "Yes!"

"So you have no interest in me except for what I've been able to do for you."

Her features hardened. "I came to you with a business proposition. You *know* how grateful I am for what you've done for me—"

"But it's all work and no play, even though you're separated from your beloved by thousands of miles?"

Those blue eyes looked haunted. "What do you want from me?"

"How about honesty."

"I'm being honest," her voice trembled.

"The hell you are—" he whispered fiercely. Having taken all he could, he pulled her close so their mouths were almost touching. "I'm feeling something I've never felt before and I know you're feeling it too, but your guilt is preventing you from admitting it. The fact that guilt is getting in the way means you couldn't possibly love this man the way you should."

A strangled moan escaped her lips.

"I'm going to kiss you, Jasmine, and then we'll know for a certainty."

Luc found her mouth and coaxed her lips apart. In the next instant he felt her begin to kiss him back with such answering hunger, it took his breath.

He'd wanted this kiss to happen for so long, and now that it had, he couldn't stop. Her passionate response took them to a deeper level until they both moaned with pleasure.

He was so far gone and so enamored of her that when she suddenly wrenched her mouth from his, it brought a protest from him.

"No more," she cried. Breathing heavily, she eased herself out of his arms. She sat back and said, "I knew deep down there would be a price to pay for your generosity that went beyond bank boundaries. Am I to presume *this* is the payment you're really after for bending your own rules to help me?"

In that second while the unexpected question caught him off guard, she moved away and got out of the car.

He stared at her through narrowed lids, making no move to stop her. "Now we know the truth, don't we? A moment ago you were right with me, kiss for kiss, and obviously feeling even more guilt about it than I realized. Otherwise a woman like you who is sacrificing everything for the good of one man and the company would never accuse me of buying you to get you in my bed.

"Need I remind you that you came to me first? In case you think your moment of righteous indignation for whatever you believe I'm guilty of has ruined everything, be assured our deal still stands. I'm a man of my word. *À bientôt*, Jasmine."

As he drove off, Luc thought he heard her

calling him back, but in his savage state of mind, he knew it safer to keep on going.

Mortified was the only word that even came close to what Jasmine experienced as she watched Luc disappear from sight. The insult she'd flung at him was unconscionable and could never be erased. The second his mouth had descended, she'd started kissing him back with a fervency she hadn't known herself capable of. But it had frightened her so terribly she'd torn her lips from his.

What kind of evil streak did she possess to kiss him as she'd done while pretending there was a man in her life? And then to turn on Luc with such cruelty because he'd guessed the truth.

Luc would never have to buy a woman. He could have any woman he wanted. He'd been honest with her about his painful loss. He'd opened up to her. That couldn't have been easy to do. In fact, he would never tell something that private to a person he didn't care about. In so many words, he'd let her know there was no significant other in his life since that terrible time.

And look what she'd done to him—

Tonight he'd wanted to kiss her. Heaven knew she'd wanted him to kiss her, but after she'd felt his mouth devouring hers, she'd been afraid it wouldn't stop there. *And not because of him.*

Jasmine wanted to crawl in a hole. Without his willing help, who knew how long it would have taken to get a bank loan somewhere else. She had to do something to fix this, but didn't know how.

Maybe he hadn't heard her call out for him to stop. If she tried phoning him right now, would he answer? He'd only been gone a few minutes.

Desperate to stop the bleeding, she pulled out her cell and pressed the digit for his number she'd programmed into her phone. To her chagrin, the call went directly to his voice mail. When she heard the prompt, the words came pouring out of her.

Another phone call had gone to Luc's voice mail. In this black mood, he didn't dare talk to anyone. It was probably his sister calling again about the party for Sunday she was planning for her husband's birthday. She wouldn't relent until he let her know he'd be there with a girlfriend.

After the dark moment with Jasmine, he wasn't fit company for anyone. Tomorrow he'd clear out for the weekend. Luc had no idea where he'd go. He only knew he had to get far away.

Further ahead of him, he saw lights flashing. There'd been an accident. He had to stop behind a line of cars. While he was forced to wait, he glanced at the caller ID on his phone. Seeing Jasmine's name there almost caused his heart to palpitate out of his chest. In the next instant, he listened to her message.

"Luc? You have to forgive me for what I said. I didn't mean it. You know I didn't."

He could hear her voice shaking over the line.

"I'm aware I don't deserve a chance to explain, but I have to. You have to let me. Please turn around and come back. I won't be able to sleep tonight until I've talked to you. You

don't need to call me. Just come. I'll wait for you. Please."

That urgent throb in her tone connected in a more powerful way than her words. He came close to causing another accident by turning around and peeling down the road toward Grasse.

The ten minutes it took to reach her house were the longest he'd ever known. He levered himself from the car and strode to the front door. As he started to knock, it opened. Jasmine's nervous expression left little to the imagination.

"I've been waiting, but I can't believe you came back. It proves what a good man you are." That was the second time she'd told him that. She opened the door wider. "Come in and we'll go out on the terrace."

He followed, watching the sway of her womanly hips as she led him through the hallway to the salon. From the French doors, they walked out to a terrace with lawn furniture. It overlooked a flower garden. He walked over to the stone balustrade. The sweetness of the blossoms intoxicated him.

"What is that smell?"

"Rose de Mai. Papa's Aunt Dominique loved this garden."

"Heavenly stuff," he murmured after turning to her. She'd perched on one end of the swing.

"You have to forgive me," she began. "I've never been intentionally rude to anyone in my life. That makes twice now with you, but I don't want you to think I'm the girl you thought I was on Yeronisos."

He lounged against the balustrade, still struggling to deal with his emotions. "In other words, I bring out something in you that makes you cross a line, is that what you're saying?"

She leaned forward with her arms on top of her legs, clasping her hands. "You didn't do anything wrong. I take full responsibility." Her head was down, causing her gleaming dark hair to slide forward. "I'd like to blame my cruelty on a nervous breakdown or temporary insanity or some such thing. But it wouldn't be the truth."

Honesty from her at last…

"I've lived a very selfish life, Luc. Been given every gift without counting the cost."

His brows furrowed. Where was she going with this?

"When you told me how you felt after the plane crash, it pressed on a nerve inside me.

"I'd always had this feeling of immortality too, that I could fit everything into the life I wanted, when I wanted. I had time for all there was to accomplish. There'd be no bell tolling for me.

"Then I woke up on my twenty-sixth birthday and realized the day had come when everything was now on my shoulders. Papa had put me in charge to carry out his wishes and trusted me not to fail. Up until then it had seemed like some dream that wasn't based in reality. But it wasn't a dream!" She lifted her head. "Suddenly I felt my mortality for the first time, and I was terrified. I still am…"

Luc knew that feeling all too well.

"It's not just the fear of failing Papa. It's the realization that I failed the parents I adore. So many missed chances that I can never recapture."

He moved closer. "I've been following you until now. What do you mean, missed chances?"

She got up from the swing. "To show them my love. I've been a selfish daughter, Luc. I— I've been as horrible to them as Paul Ferrier was to his son." Her voice faltered. "I neglected them by putting my interests first. Papa was such a fascinating figure, I loved being with him. In the process, my father took a back seat without my meaning for it to happen. He and Mother made it so easy for me. *Too* easy. I see that now."

"Aren't you being too hard on yourself? I'm sure your parents recognized you had a special destiny. A good parent enables their child to live up to her full potential."

Her face was a study in pain. "Even so, I recognize what I've done and want to make it up to them. My siblings have always been there for them when I was nowhere around."

Luc was beginning to put all the pieces together. "So now you're going home to live and make things right."

"If it isn't too late to repair the damage."

"Jasmine—there's no damage. Your case isn't anything like that of the prodigal son. You had their blessing. When you spent so much time in France, you didn't turn your back on them or fritter away your inheritance."

"But in a sense I did, Luc! I left my father's home and the life he'd planned with Mother for *our* family." She started to sob. "I'm worse than Paul Ferrier."

Without conscious thought, Luc reached out to crush her guilt-ridden body in his arms. "Hush," he murmured into her hair. He'd finally gotten the truth out of her. There was no man waiting for her. But the realization had thrown him into a new quandary.

Luc could have handled that form of competition. But he had a much greater adversary in the form of her father, whom she now wanted to shower with love for the rest of her life. That meant her leaving France for good.

If she were to get involved with Luc, he'd be the one standing in her way. That's why she'd said something hurtful to him when he'd known in his gut it was totally out of character for her. Luc had found out that when Jasmine did something, she went at it with all the energy of her soul.

He got it.

This was a moral dilemma staring him in the face on a whole new scale. Luc didn't know if he had the fortitude to do the right thing and walk away. But if he continued to feel her beautiful body pressed against his, he'd start to make love to her.

Do you want to take the chance that she'll say something hurtful again and mean it this time, Charriere? Do you want your life to be utterly destroyed by loving this woman whose destiny lies on the other side of the world? Get away while you can.

To his dismay, she must have been reading his mind because she eased away from him first and hugged her arms to her waist. "Thank you for giving me the chance to explain."

Luc took a deep breath. "You're under a tremendous amount of stress. I'm going to leave so you can get to bed." *Get out of there before you're tempted beyond endurance.* "If you need me for anything, call me. Good night, Jasmine."

He left her standing on the terrace and hurried out to his car. This time she didn't call him back. How in the name of all that was holy was he going to handle it?

CHAPTER SEVEN

THE DAY OF the board meeting had finally arrived. The Ferrier members on the board hadn't been at all happy about her bringing the date forward to Friday, but so far none of them had formed a mutiny. Everyone had assembled in the conference room of the perfumery.

She'd found it hard to sleep since Luc had left La Tourette a week ago. His brilliant mind had figured out what she'd been trying to tell him. So far he hadn't phoned her. She'd known he wouldn't, but it devastated her to the point she felt ill.

Over the last week she'd spent all her time with Remy. They'd planned he would stay out in the reception area with his family until she called for him to come into the room and be introduced to the board. Remy had been amazing through it all.

He knew the board might not vote for him, but Jasmine could see he was handling it because her grandfather's ghost had been laid to rest for good. Getting back the house and the estate where he'd grown up had made a huge difference in him. Jasmine knew he would go on being a flower farmer and helping his family, but with one difference. He'd be happy.

Before she walked in the conference room, she said a little prayer. "I've done everything I could, Papa. The rest is no longer in my hands."

Squaring her shoulders, she entered the room and walked to the head of the long conference table. Giles LeClos sat on her left, Roger Ferrier, her oldest uncle, on her right. Her eyes traveled around the table, lighting on her relatives and staff members, all fourteen of them.

None of them had been able to accept the fact that their father and grandfather had chosen her. She knew the feelings of resentment, even anger against his choice, had been roiling inside of them and she understood.

"I can't thank you enough for dropping everything to be here this afternoon. Some of you had to fly from Paris. If it weren't of the most vital importance, I wouldn't have called for a meeting even earlier than planned." Several of her family sent each other off-putting silent messages.

"I'll make this short. First of all, I've made the decision not to be associated with the company any longer. Secondly, I won't be working as a nose anymore. I'm moving back to the States for good."

A collective gasp reverberated in the room. They stared at her like they'd seen a ghost.

"However, I'm leaving you in the hands of the only person who has the right to run this company as he sees fit. There would be no company to run if it weren't for the genius of this man, who did everything his father never could. I'm talking about Paul Ferrier's son and heir, Remy Ferrier."

A strange silence enveloped the room.

If Jasmine had announced the end of the world, she doubted the reaction would have

been any different. "Giles? Please give everyone a file that contains all the pertinent information they need to see on Remy. While you
do that, I'll ask Remy to come in. He's right
outside."

The other man looked shocked, but he did her
bidding. She went to the doors and beckoned to
Remy. He came in and stood next to her. She
squeezed his hand and introduced him to everyone; then she nodded to her grandfather's
attorney. "Please read the part of Papa's will
none of you have heard yet."

Her heart was pounding furiously as the
older man stood up and put on his glasses. "Beloved family and staff members—Remy was
the brother I never had. I loved him." Jasmine
squeezed his hand again and never let go. "He
should have run the company from the start,
but it wasn't meant to be while Paul was alive
and insisted that I run things.

"After he died, I begged Remy to come back
and run the company, but by then he had other
interests. It is my wish that he be installed now.

I've used my sweet granddaughter Jasmine shamelessly to make this happen.

"You who are my children and grandchildren have all been wonderful stewards of the company. So has my faithful staff. No one could have asked for better. But no one has the right to head Ferriers except the man who worked in the trenches of the company as a boy and knows every jot and tittle of what makes it tick.

"With Remy's vision, he'll do miraculous things that will put the company on top and stay there. Be his friend. Accept his guidance. Remy has a reputation among the work force of our company in the Midi. When they hear he's been installed, you'll see them wearing a smile again because he's one of them. In no time at all you'll find out that Ferriers has a weapon like no other."

Jasmine had been watching their faces during the reading. The whole demeanor of the room had changed. They acted like they were in a trance.

For a sixty-six-year-old man, Remy looked

younger and sensational in an olive suit with a light green shirt and tie. He'd worked in the fields most of his life when he wasn't racing or drinking. Besides having an amazing physique with no fat on him, he was still handsome and bronzed by the sun. Naturally, he'd aged, but his dark red hair was still vibrant and thick.

She smiled at him. "We'd all like to hear from you, Remy."

He kissed her cheek. "I can see we're all in shock," he quipped. "Max and I grew up under the same roof and were like brothers, being only two years apart. I remember a time when a rival in the perfume industry caused an explosion at the lab in Hyeres. By now, my father was dead and it was right before Max got married.

"Everyone thought the act of sabotage had killed him. During that horrendous time when we couldn't find his body, I felt like I wanted to die. That's when I realized what his life meant to me. We can thank God he wasn't killed. You've all heard stories and rumors, some true, some not. The fact is, he and I went through hell and back together, but in the end, we're still brothers.

"Like my psychiatrist told me when I went to him for my former drinking problem, he told me that unless I was willing to work with him, then there was no reason for me to continue seeing him. That's my speech to you. If you're willing to work with me, I'll do everything I can to earn your trust."

Jasmine grabbed his arm. "His Parma violets will be the envy of every perfume house. For the last year, I've worked on a perfume with essential oil from the violets he's been growing.

"He's the only person in the world to grow this variety, and thousands more are going to be planted. He calls them Reine Fleury. As you know, Remy's mother's name was Rosaline Fleury. I've given each of you a tiny sample bottle of perfume to open now."

In a few minutes the room smelled like a garden of violets. The sounds of *ahs* and pleasure from everyone told the story as nothing else could.

"When this perfume is out on the market, it will turn the company's revenues around. With that said, I propose we now take a vote by secret ballot."

Remy excused himself and left the room.

"I'm going to vote my conscience and know you will do the same. Giles? If you'll start the process."

A few minutes later, Giles read the verdict. "The vote is unanimous in favor of Remy Ferrier."

Your dream came true, Papa.

Jasmine ran to the door and asked Remy and his family to come in. When they entered, everyone stood up and started clapping. She could hardly see the green of his eyes for the tears in her own. She hugged him hard. "It was unanimous. Welcome home, dear Remy."

Everyone gathered round him and his family to shake their hands and congratulate him.

Unable to stand it any longer, she whispered, "Do you mind if I leave you for a little while?

You're in good hands. I'll meet you back at the house later."

"Where are you going?"

"I need to see the man who made all this possible."

Jasmine flew out of the perfumery as if her feet had wings.

En route she phoned her parents and told them the joyous news. "Everything I wanted to do for Papa has been accomplished. It won't be long before I'm home for good. I love you both so much, you can't imagine."

Luc couldn't concentrate. He'd stayed away from Jasmine for the last week and had been in hell. He knew the board meeting at the perfumery had been called for today. He checked his watch. Three-thirty. Though he'd promised himself he wouldn't do it, at some point he knew he was going to break down and phone her.

He had one more phone conference with the branch manager in Colle-sur-Loup, but he couldn't bring himself to deal with business right now.

"Thomas? Get Emil Rocher on the phone for me and tell him we'll have to do the conference tomorrow. I'm leaving for home now." He stood up to leave.

"You can't go home yet."

"Why not?"

"You've another appointment waiting for you out here."

"Tell them I'm sorry, but they'll have to schedule for another day."

"I don't think you want me to do that. She's on her way in now."

The main door to his office opened. "Luc?"

Jasmine's excited cry sent adrenaline flooding through his system as she hurried inside and paused a few feet away from his desk. Her eyes glowed like sapphires.

"It worked! Everything worked. Remy's the new CEO by unanimous vote. It's because of you that any of this happened! Can we go somewhere private to talk so I can thank you? Do you have time?"

Luc looked into her face beaming with happiness. "What do you think?" he said fiercely. "We're going for a boat ride and you can tell me everything. We'll drive back for your car later."

There was no argument from her as he hustled her through the rear door and they climbed in his car. Luc's cruiser was moored at the main boat dock for easy access two miles away. The drive only took a few minutes. He left the car in the parking area and they walked along the floating dock to his cabin cruiser.

After handing her a life jacket, he removed his suit jacket and tie. Once he'd rolled up his shirtsleeves, he undid the ropes and idled the boat at wake speed. When they'd cleared the buoys, he opened it up and they flew across the blue water away from shore.

To be with her like this had lit him on fire. The fact that she'd come running to him instead of phoning him with the news proved she was on fire for him too. Right now, he refused to think about her leaving France. She was here on his boat. She was with him. Nothing else mattered. No tomorrows. This time was for them.

The sun made the sea air balmy. Now that they were away from people, he cut the motor. "Come and sit in the back of the boat with me." They made their way to the seats.

Jasmine had worn a pale pink two-piece suit with short sleeves to the meeting. Between her coloring and her outfit, she looked good enough to eat. She tucked one leg under her and turned to face him. He stretched his arm along the top of the seatback near her.

"I want to hear it all from the beginning. Don't leave anything out."

She brushed some strands of hair out of her eyes. "Luc? I meant what I said earlier. None of this would have been possible without you. It got Remy there. Then the attorney read part of Papa's will no one had heard yet. In it, he paid tribute to Remy, the man he'd loved like a brother. The words were so touching, there wasn't a dry eye in the room."

Hers had filled with tears. "It *was* a far, far better thing you did for him than anyone else has ever done for him before. Thank you doesn't begin to express what's in my heart, but I'll say it again anyway." She leaned closer and kissed his cheek. "Thank you, thank you, thank you," she cried until he couldn't hold back his hunger.

Seven days apart had been too long. Luc had needed to feel her mouth moving beneath his again. He covered those lips, smothering the words, and there was no more talk. The taste of her was a revelation. Time had no meaning as each kiss deepened and lasted longer.

She gave freely, thrilling him to the core. He'd been with other women, but he'd never known ecstasy like this. Cradling her face, he brushed his lips relentlessly over every lovely feature, so precious to him. "You're incredibly beautiful, Jasmine. I'm sure you've heard that all your life, but I've seen inside the part of you that hides the secret of your beauty. It comes from your soul. I didn't know anyone like you existed."

They kissed again with a devouring hunger

neither could hide. "Because of your faith in me, I could say the same thing about you. As I told you the other night, you're a good man." Her eyes burned like blue flames. "Do you have any idea how rare you are?"

He kissed her back, longer and harder. But he couldn't get close enough to her while she was wearing the life jacket. "I'm going to drive us to that little cove you can see from here where we won't be bothered by the wakes from other boats. Stay right there and don't move. Promise?"

"I promise, but where would I go?" Her breathing sounded shallow.

Somehow, he didn't know how, he left her long enough to drive them the short distance to a stretch of beach. He cut the motor and the hull glided on to the sand. With his heart pumping too fast, Luc walked back to her.

"Let's take off that preserver so I can get my arms around you properly."

She undid it before he could help and threw it on the floor. A little smile lifted one corner of her delectable mouth when she said, "Now I'm going to find out just how difficult it would have been to save your unconscious body after your rental boat crashed into a shark."

He pulled her into his arms. Finally there was no space separating them.

Her eyes melted into his. "You know something? You're a lot more man than I realized, Luc Charriere, and gorgeous besides. So gorgeous I have a hard time taking my eyes off of you. Thank heaven you weren't killed in that plane crash." Her voice shook. "Then we would never have met, and you wouldn't have made me the happiest woman alive today."

His breath caught. "I know what getting Remy that loan has meant to you."

"That's true, but you know very well I'm talking about you and the way you make me feel. I thought my problems would be over once he was installed, but now I discover I've got a bigger problem."

"What's that?"

"You." A tortured sigh escaped her throat. "What am I going to do about you?"

A charge ignited his body. "What do you *want* to do?"

"I have my dreams, but they can't come true, so there's no point in talking about them. I've got to be content with what I have right here, right now, with you."

This time, she searched for his mouth with stunning impatience, telling him without words. Their kiss went on and on until he felt transported.

But a different kind of pain than he'd known before shot through him because this was her goodbye kiss. He pulled her right up against his chest and buried his face in her neck. She really was going away. This wasn't something he could talk her out of.

"Jasmine? Before you leave for the States, I have to spend some time with you. I'll take my vacation now. How soon do you have to go?"

"I promised to be home on August seventh.

It's my parents' thirtieth wedding anniversary party."

So soon? Everything in him rebelled. His mind calculated the time. "That gives us a week."

A moan sounded before she moved off his lap and stood up. "No more make-believe, Luc. I couldn't go anywhere with you."

He stared up at her. "Why not?"

"You *know* why. Your life is here. Mine is on the other side of the Atlantic. How could it possibly be good for either of us to go off for that long, knowing we're going to say good-bye at the end? The thought of it is too painful to even contemplate." Her voice throbbed. "At least it is for me. But you're a man, so it's different for you."

"Explain that remark."

Jasmine wouldn't look at him. "You can go away with a woman and enjoy the time thoroughly. When it's over you can move on. But women are different. Not all, but some. *I'm* different. To travel and make love with you, only to get on a plane at the end of that journey and wave goodbye, sounds like a kind of purgatory I have no desire to live through."

He grasped her hand. "Then we won't sleep together."

She looked down at him and smiled. "You're a Frenchman, aren't you?"

"I'm a man like all other men, and the thought of making love to you has been on my mind since I saw you on Yeronisos. But that isn't why I want to go away with you. If you think making love to you is all I'm after, then you have an odd conception about me.

"The other day I told you I have feelings for you I've never had for another woman. If all I can do is hold you and kiss you while we're on vacation, it will be enough. What I'd truly regret is not being able to get to know Jasmine Martin, the fabulous woman inside the girl who makes me want to be a better man."

"*Luc.*"

"It's true. Is life so cut and dried and riddled with deadlines, we can't take time out for ourselves to feed our own needs? The cruiser sleeps two comfortably and can go anywhere on the Mediterranean. We'll explore grottos and ruins. While you're still in France I can indulge in *my* dreams. I have them too, you know."

She looked shocked. "You really could get away now?"

He got to his feet. "My work will still be here when I get back. You *won't* be. We've cleared up all the business there is to do. Now I want to spend every second possible with you not worrying about anything or anyone but each other."

"I want that too," she admitted at last. "But I can't be gone a whole week. I have a few more preparations to make before I leave."

That was all he needed to hear. Now that Luc could breathe again, he had to think fast. He handed her the life preserver to put on. "Let's pick up your car and I'll follow you to Grasse. Once you've packed a bag, we'll come back in my car. I'll gather my things and we'll set off in the cruiser. When we find a spot we like, we'll lay anchor for the night."

Taking advantage of her silence, he walked to the forward part of the cruiser and jumped to the sand to push it into the water.

He should have followed her up that cliff last May. They might still be on Cyprus, too enthralled with each other to care about anything else. But there was no point in looking back. The next few days were what counted. He couldn't think beyond that.

Several hours later Jasmine sat across from Luc as they skimmed the water along the Italian coast in the sleek white, seaworthy cruiser. "See those lights ahead?" She nodded. "Now that we've passed Alassio, we're coming to Baba Beach, where we're going to spend the night. It won't be crowded."

With Luc, she was going to see the charming delights along the Cote d'Azur she hadn't had time to explore while she'd been working. The scene ahead looked like fairyland.

He pulled into a protected bay. She saw a sailboat farther on, but Luc had been right. They were virtually alone. Once he'd dropped anchor near the shore, she removed her life preserver. At the house, she'd changed into jeans and a top. It was still warm out so she didn't need a jacket yet.

Luc had dressed in sweats and a T-shirt. On their way to the pier, he'd driven her to his villa near the Grimaldi castle in Cagnes-sur-Mer, a medieval town with a warren of alleyways and decorated wooden doors. Flowers abounded and cascaded from the balconies. It was a dream home. This had been the hometown of the Charrieres for generations. She'd been enchanted.

He propped a couple of loungers side by side on the deck. "What do you say we relax for a while before going downstairs to bed?"

"Ooh, yes! Who could go to sleep yet on a night like this?"

His eyes smiled at her. "Want a soda?" Luc was attentive to her every need. Jasmine had dated a little in college, but hardly at all in the last two years. She'd almost forgotten what it was like to be waited on and pampered.

"Not right now, thanks. What about you?"

"I'm perfect," he murmured.

They'd stopped for dinner on the way back from Grasse and had bought some food and drinks to stow on board. Right now, they had everything they needed.

She lay down on her stomach with her face turned toward the beach. Luc stretched out on his side facing her with his hand propping his dark head. Jasmine chuckled. "You're turned the wrong way."

"I've been here before and am seeing the sight I want."

Everything he said filled her with warmth. "You're terrible."

"You're breathtaking. My grandfather had a copy of your grandmother's book in his library. I've read it and looked at all the pictures. You're more beautiful than she was and have the coloring of your grandfather. The combination is startling. Remy must have been shocked to see you face to face."

Jasmine turned on her side. "I know he was."

"Tell me the other reason besides pride that kept him from coming back to run the company after his father died. I know it had to do with your grandmother."

Nothing got past Luc. She took a deep breath. "Do you remember when I told you that he went to Paris to run the company while my grandfather was on a trip to South America?"

"I do, but I didn't know he'd gone so far away."

"After his first wife and unborn baby died, the doctor told him to take a long trip."

Luc sat up. "I didn't know about a baby."

"Not many people do. It would have been his firstborn. He had a few friends who enjoyed archaeology the way he did, so he joined them. Before leaving, he asked Remy to go to Paris and run the company. While Remy was there, he wanted him to attend the annual perfume awards banquet with the staff. Papa was glad to get out of it."

"That's right. He hated publicity."

She nodded. "Remy went. It was held at the Hotel de Ville. Everyone who was anyone was there, including the president of France and some famous film stars like Yves Montand and Simone Signoret. While they stopped by the Ferrier table to talk to Remy, a woman bumped into him by accident, causing the champagne he'd been drinking to stain his ruffled shirt. That woman was my grandmother, Megan Hunt."

"Why was she there?"

"Henri Brescault, a reporter for the *Paris-Soir*, was covering the event for the paper. He was hoping to get an interview with my grandfather, who kept winning the perfume award year after year. This reporter had a sister who was best friends with my grandmother. The uncle who raised her after her parents were killed was an Egyptologist and had given her a necklace that predated Christ."

"You're joking."

"No. He worked at the Peabody Institute. Anyway, Henri asked her to wear it because he'd heard my grandfather would be in attendance. He hoped the necklace would catch Papa's attention and garner him an interview."

Luc smiled. "But nothing worked as planned because Maxim wasn't there."

"That's right. Remy took one look at her and fell madly in love. She'd just graduated as a translator from the Sorbonne. He didn't want to lose her to a job in England, so he begged his Aunt Dominique to hire her to help at the boarding school she ran in Switzerland. The night he asked her to marry him, she told him she cared for him very much, but she wasn't ready to commit to marriage yet.

"In his pain, he drove off and got into a car accident with his Porsche. He ended up in the hospital. He was supposed to have driven her to Switzerland the next day. Unbeknownst to him, my grandfather returned from his trip a week earlier than planned because his aunt hadn't been well and he was worried about her. When he walked into his apartment in Paris, he received a call from Remy, who was still in the hospital. Remy had thought the apartment retainer would answer, but it was my grandfather.

"Remy told Papa he'd fallen in love and was planning to be married at Christmas. Remy led Papa to believe he and my grandmother were engaged, which of course they weren't. As a favor, he asked Papa to please pick up my grandmother at her apartment and drive her to the train leaving for Switzerland early the next morning."

Luc shook his head.

"It was the perfect storm. Instead of putting her on the train, Papa drove her to Lausanne because he intended to drop in on his aunt, who'd already promised him she would close the school and stay home in Grasse.

"On the drive, he found out my grandmother wasn't engaged and the two of them fell so deeply in love they didn't know what to do. After Remy recovered from his accident, he discovered what had happened and his heart was broken beyond repair. He went after Papa in Grasse. They had a literal physical fight before Remy left for Paris and never came back home."

"So the rest was history?" Luc surmised.

"Yes. My grandmother was in Switzerland when she found out about the fight. Knowing she was the cause of it horrified her because she loved Remy too, but not the way she loved Papa. In despair she left for the States, where neither man could ever find her, hoping that if she disappeared, the two of them could mend their differences. But Papa hunted her down until he found her in Driggs, Idaho, where she'd been born. They got married there and he brought her back to Grasse."

"Mon Dieu."

Jasmine sat up. "Perhaps now you understand why Papa suffered so much grief. Not only was Paul's cruelty unforgiveable, Remy saw my grandparents' love affair as a great betrayal. Neither Papa nor my grandmother meant for any of it to happen.

"If you want to know the truth, before my grandmother died, she confided in me about

Remy. The things she loved about him touched my heart. Papa wasn't the only one who suffered. Grandma wanted to love Remy the way a woman loves a man. She tried so hard. In fact, she admitted to me that if she'd never met my grandfather, she would probably have ended up marrying Remy.

"For nights, I listened to her tell me about their love story. He was so good to her while she was studying for her finals. Remy was prepared to give her the world. During those talks, I felt so close to him. Between my grandparents' confidences about him, I felt like I knew him even though I hadn't met him. I truly love him. Do you find that strange?"

"Not at all." She could tell by Luc's expression he'd been moved. "But it would take a strong man to overcome that kind of emotional pain."

"Still, it didn't break him, and Papa knew it. That's why he begged me to help Remy. Grandma begged me too."

He stared at her. "You have a look of your

grandmother. It must have been like déjà vu for him when you showed up in his violet field."

"That's exactly what I thought when he turned around and saw me. I never prayed so hard in my life for a miracle to happen."

"I had no idea so much was at stake. You've carried a heavy load."

"Which you lightened by listening to me and helping me. I'm so thankful for you, Luc." She could feel tears smarting her eyelids. "Enough talk about my life. I want to hear about the girl you loved. Tell me about her."

Lines darkened his handsome features. "Sabine's family moved to Cagnes from Paris our senior year. She was different from the other girls I knew."

"In what way?"

"She was funny, and fun. I was intrigued and invited her to hang out with me and my best friend, Philippe. A group of us did all sorts of crazy things when we weren't studying. She fit right in."

Jasmine smiled. "Define crazy."

"My parents labeled me a daredevil at an early age. That's what we did. We dared each other to push the envelope, no matter what it was."

"Like the guys on the island."

He nodded.

"Were you lovers?"

"Yes."

His answer shouldn't have hurt, but it did.

"We were crazy about each other. I got this idea that after we graduated from high school, we'd get married and take my sailboat around the world. You know. Stop for a while here and there to earn a little money, then move on to the next stop.

"Considering that my family had their own specific dreams for me, they would have been horrified if they'd known what I'd planned. But a selfish eighteen-year-old isn't thinking about anyone else."

Remembered pain seeped in. "I was the same way, Luc. Without giving my parents' wishes a thought, I wanted to go to the Sorbonne, where my grandparents had gone." She shook her head. "Forgive me for interrupting you. Go on," she urged.

"There isn't anything else. The day we graduated, we decided to go skydiving. It was my idea. Our big adventure sounded like the perfect way to start the summer. We took off in a single-engine plane near Cannet-des-Maures. One minute, we were all laughing and getting ready to parachute. In the next minute, the plane lost power and we plowed into a hill."

He got up from the lounger and walked over to the side of the cruiser. In agony for him, she jumped up and joined him. "I can't imagine the horror of it. Were you in the hospital a long time?"

"Three months with a bruised spine. My parents and grandparents never left me alone. At first, the doctors didn't think I'd ever walk again. At the time, I didn't care. I'd lost Sabine. It was my fault she and Philippe were dead. I wanted to die."

Luc was no stranger to guilt of the worst kind.

"Surely you still don't blame yourself? You couldn't have known that plane would crash."

"You're right, but it took me a long time to throw off the burden."

She studied him for a moment. "I'm so sorry for your suffering."

He wrapped his arms around her and rocked her in place for a long time. "It all happened a long time ago. I haven't talked about it for years."

Jasmine lifted a hand and caressed the side of his hard jaw. "I shouldn't have brought it up."

"I'm glad you did." He kissed her fingertips.

"How did you pull out of your morose state?"

"My physical therapist told me he was being replaced. I asked him why. He said that when there were other patients fighting to get better, he couldn't work with one who had a death wish. Since the doctor had given me the prognosis of a full recovery if I worked hard, he found me utterly selfish and pathetic and refused to waste his time."

"Oh, Luc—"

"'Oh, Luc' is right. When he walked out on me, I got angry. That was the first real emotion to wake me up to my sickening state of mind. In another six months, I could walk with a cane. A year later, I'd thrown it away and started university at Sophia Antipolis in Nice where I took courses in economics and management.

"It was there I made good friends with Nic Valfort. We both went to graduate school in Paris. Life got better from that point on. Speaking of Nic, he has invited me to his house on Saturday evening and wants me to bring someone. When we get back from our trip, I'd like you to go with me. You'll enjoy his wife, Laura, who's your age. She's from San Francisco."

"An American? That's interesting. But I'm not sure if I'll have time. My flight leaves the next day."

"Then we'll make sure you find the time. He saw you on TV and wants to meet the famous head of Ferriers."

"After today, I'm no longer anything. That's

the trouble with fame. Here today, gone tomorrow," she quipped.

Luc winced, not able to appreciate the humor when he knew she was going to leave him. He walked her back over to the loungers. "I don't want to talk about tomorrow. We came on this trip to get to know each other better. I want to hear about all the various men in your life."

She sank back down. "You make it sound like there have been legions."

He sat opposite her, tracing the outline of her cheek with his finger. "I have no doubt legions of men have desired you, but I want to know about the one or two who were lucky enough to enjoy your company."

"I dated some in high school, mostly group dates. But there was one guy named Hank Branson."

He grinned. "Sounds like a cowboy."

She nodded. "The year I met him I was seventeen. Dad had taken the family to the rodeo. My father was a famous bull rider at one time and he's always had an active association with the

rodeo. Both my brothers got into it for a while. They became friends with Hank, an eighteen-year-old steer wrestler from Rexburg, a town a half hour away. I was introduced to him.

"In the arena he was known as Hank the Tank because he was big and tough. And cute.

"Every girl around was nuts about him. I was smitten. When he took time off, he came by the house during the year while I was home. I was in heaven riding around the ranch with him, going out on the occasional steak fry with him and our family.

"We went to movies and did some hiking in the Tetons. He gave me my first kiss and told me he was going to marry me when I was all grown up. We dated on and off for about three years, but because I spent so much time in France, it was hit and miss.

"The family really liked him, and dad kept telling me I couldn't do any better. Hank has gone into business with his father, who owns a big, successful ranch. They're good people. But at one point I realized my crush on him had worn off. When he brought up marriage again, I had to tell him I wasn't in love with him and that ended it."

Luc closed his eyes. "The poor devil," he muttered, once again stunned by the revelations falling from her lips. "Are you sure he's still not waiting for you when you go home?"

"For his sake, I hope not."

"What about the men you met at the university in Paris?"

"I went out with several guys, but I never had a lover if that's what you're asking."

Never? "Surely there must have been someone who mattered to you."

"There was one named André. We dated some until I realized he was too dictatorial. He tried to order me around."

"You mean the way I did to you on the island?"

She nodded. "For a few moments, you reminded me of him."

"So that's why you were so angry with me."

"Only for a moment, Luc. Now you know

about my legions of love affairs. I'm afraid I've put you to sleep."

"If anything, it's your voice that sounds tired. Maybe we ought to head downstairs. I think I've worn you out after all that's happened today."

He pulled her along with him and they went below. To her surprise, he didn't linger in the doorway to her cabin.

"I need to put the boat to bed. So you'll feel safe, I'll turn on the cruiser's warning device. Sleep well." After a brief kiss to her lips, he walked back toward the stairs, leaving her with an ache that would keep her awake all night.

CHAPTER EIGHT

As SHE GOT READY, Jasmine realized she wasn't on Luc's mind right now. How could she be after she'd forced him to relive his tragic past? But she was glad she knew. The experience had helped him to become the remarkable man he was today. *The man you're going to leave after this short vacation is over.*

In order not to think about that, she took out a map of the Mediterranean he'd given her to study and got in bed. Tomorrow he'd let her pick their next spot to explore. Jasmine couldn't recall ever having had this kind of joy in her life. There was only one reason why. *Luc.*

But he was probably up on deck recalling his former dream of sailing around the world. Unfortunately, his dream had been dashed. Jasmine shuddered and tried to focus on their destination for tomorrow, but that didn't work.

After studying the map for a while longer, she fell asleep. She came awake the next morning with a pounding heartbeat. Nothing could slow down her heartbeat knowing Luc was on board. After a shower, she dressed in a plum-colored bikini. When she'd put on a matching beach wrap, she went up on deck to find him.

"Luc?"

"There's my Amazon warrior. I'm out here!"

With a chuckle, she turned in time to see his dark, handsome head while he treaded water. "Come on in! It's the perfect temperature."

Jasmine needed to tie back her hair first, but that meant going below. His invitation was so inviting, she forgot about it and made her way to the transom. Then, removing her wrap, she dove into the brilliant blue water. He swam toward her. The sight of him with his black hair slicked back and those jet-black eyes devouring her thrilled her so much it was hard to breathe.

He reached for her hand and drew her into him. "I've been waiting for my breakfast and here you are." His white smile was devilish. "I'm not sure which part of you I want to eat first."

Jasmine laughed nervously until he captured her mouth and twirled them around. Having lived by the water all his life, Luc swam like a fish. He kept them buoyant as he turned on his back with her lying on top of him so they could drink deeply of each other. They played and kissed both in and on top of the water. For a while, she lost all sense of time, never wanting sensual pleasure like this to end.

Though going to bed with a man was one experience she hadn't known yet, Luc was teaching her ways to enjoy the exquisite pleasure of being with a man. Nothing in life had prepared her for happiness like this. He lifted her high above the water while he turned in circles. When he lowered her again, his eyes played over her hair.

"Do you know the individual strands sparkle in the sunlight like there are little jewels in them? I never saw anything like it."

Her heart quivered. "When I was a little girl, my dad told me the same thing. From that point on, he called me Sparkles."

Luc bunched her hair in his hands. "It's beautiful, just like you." After kissing it, he found her mouth once more and kissed her with an urgency that carried her away. At the height of her excitement, he said, "If I keep you out here much longer, I'm going to eat you alive." The glitter of desire in his eyes melted her insides. "Since I made you a promise, we'd better go back to the cruiser quick and find me something else to eat."

She groaned in disappointment, but knew he was right. Together, they headed for the end of the boat. He paced himself to stay with her. The feeling of oneness couldn't be described in words. It was too overpowering for that.

He climbed on the transom first, then pulled her up. She reached for her wrap and followed him on to the deck. Luc stopped at the top of the stairs to look at her. "While I put the food on the table, why don't you get the map and show me where you'd like to go."

Jasmine hurried to her room and secured her hair with an elastic. After putting on a T-shirt and shorts, she joined him in the galley and made the coffee. In a few minutes, they were poring over the chart of the Mediterranean while they ate.

"I'd like to head for Palmaria island if it's all right with you. My grandmother told me there's the most fantastic beach, but you can only reach it by boat. She also mentioned a cave."

He nodded. "Pozzale. I haven't been there in years. We should be there by early afternoon. It's the perfect place to swim in crystal-clear turquoise water and explore the caves."

"There's more than one?"

Luc flashed her a smile that sent a shockwave through her. "The side of the island in the Gulf of La Spezia faces west toward the open sea. It has high cliffs that overhang the water, in which there are many caves. You're going to love it."

She discovered that she loved doing anything

with him. When this vacation was over, she would never be the same again. By coming with him, she'd crossed a line and was playing with fire, but she couldn't help it.

"I can't wait. Let's get going. I'll do the dishes, then join you."

He got up and planted a kiss on the side of her neck. "Don't be too long. I'm already lonely without you."

So was she, at the thought of never being with him again.

Three hours later, Luc weighed anchor and together they swam to the beach. "What do you think?" he asked Jasmine, clasping her hand as they reached the sand.

"Look at all these polished pebbles! They're fantastic! This whole place is unreal!"

"It's very unique with its unspoiled natural landscape and rocky backdrop."

"I want to find some to take home to my nieces and nephews." And one for herself to remember this day.

"I'll help you take them back to the cruiser,

then I'm going to show you the Blue Cave while there aren't any tourists around. You'll understand the reason for its name when you see it."

For the next half hour, she studied the pebbles until she found the ones she wanted. Then they swam back to the boat. In another few minutes, he drove them around to the north side of the rocks. As they rounded a curve, they came to the cave opening.

She gasped. "Luc—I've never seen such a heavenly blue color."

"It's almost as heavenly as your eyes. During your television interview, they glowed like hot blue stars."

Jasmine was afraid to look at him. She feared that to spend much more time like this with him was the greatest mistake she would ever make and she would suffer for it for the rest of her life. "Can we swim in?"

"Of course. But not too far because I want to take you past another cave you'll find even more interesting."

The fun of entering the cave via the water was

only eclipsed by their journey to the next cave Luc called the Grotta dei Colombi. Translated, it was the *Cave of Pigeons.*

"You have to descend by ropes, but you need a guide. In this cave, they've found fossilized bones of Pleistocene animals. I have a feeling your grandmother explored this cave with your grandfather."

"I'm sure you're right."

"If you're ready, I'll drive us around to the civilized side of the island and we can explore before it gets too dark."

One adventure after another awaited her as Luc dropped anchor and they swam ashore to do a little exploring through the broom.

"Um...I can smell sage."

He put his arm around her waist and hugged her to his side. "With a nose like yours, I'm not surprised. Do you have any idea what those trees are ahead of us?"

They walked closer to see red-orange balls among flowers on the evergreen leaves. Jasmine couldn't believe it. "This side of the island is covered with strawberry trees! I've got to taste one."

"You're sure you want to do that?"

"Absolutely. They're edible. I'm curious about the essential oil." She bit into one then made a face. "It's very bland."

Luc laughed. "Not as tasty as a regular strawberry?"

"Not quite." She pulled another one off for him. "Are you game?"

"Try me."

She put it to his mouth and he took a bite. "It's mealy too. I think it's time to get back to the boat and fix dinner, but I want another kiss first."

Jasmine knew she'd remember this kiss, this moment, for the rest of her life. She clung to him against a setting Mediterranean sun, enjoying the taste and scent of him, including the hint of strawberry on their lips.

By the time they'd finished eating, night had fallen. Luc pulled into a small protected bay and set the anchor. It had been a hot day, but the light breeze off the water cooled them enough to make the air perfection. He placed the extended loungers side by side again and stretched out on one of them.

But when Jasmine came up on deck, she propped hers forward and sat down. He sensed she had something serious on her mind. In the dim light from the boat's navigational system, her features looked more severe. "What's wrong?" he whispered.

She stared at him. "This."

He sighed and sat up. "It's been a perfect day."

"I know," she whispered back. "Too perfect. I can't do this anymore."

"Do what?"

"Be with you."

A grimace marred his features. "In other words, you've had enough of me."

Jasmine rubbed her arms. "I wish I'd phoned you the good news about Remy and left things alone. I was out of my mind to burst into your office, and then think I could take a vacation with you before leaving France without paying a huge price.

"Please don't misunderstand. You haven't once stepped out of bounds with me. Just the opposite in fact. But it's already a painful situation for me and needs to end. I'd like to return to Cagnes-sur-Mer tomorrow."

Lines bracketed his mouth. "Even if it pains me?"

"Luc—it's no use," she blurted. "I wish there were a drink of forgetfulness so I could fly home with no memories of any kind. But that's not reality. You know I'll never forget you, so to spend even one more minute with you will only make things that much worse." She sprang from the lounger. "We haven't known each other that long, but whatever it is I'm feeling, it'll tear me apart if I don't get away from you as soon as possible."

"What about the party at Nic's on Saturday night?"

"I don't think it's a good idea. I need to sever

all ties with you. I don't want to meet your friends or your family. It's better this way."

His anger flared. He got up from the lounger and put his hands on her shoulders. "Why would you say that?"

"You *know* why! You're the CEO of the biggest bank in the South of France. Your life is here. Your family is here. My life is there with my family. I'm afraid if I don't go home now, I could lose their love. Being with you simply can't work. That dreadful cliché about ships passing in the night describes our situation. Please let me go. This isn't getting us anywhere." Her eyes had taken on a haunted cast.

"You want to go back that badly?" He almost hissed the words.

"Yes, because I don't trust myself with you any longer."

He slowly exhaled before releasing her. There was more than one way to fight this battle, but this wasn't the time. "If that's what you want, then we'll leave now. Go down to bed. By morning we'll back in Cagnes-sur-Mer and I'll drive you home."

Her face had gone pale. "Luc—" She was swallowing hard. "I'm sorry. So sorry."

"Don't be. I've enjoyed every second we've spent together. It's been a thrill, but it will have to be enough. *Bonne nuit, chérie.*"

The moment she disappeared below deck, he pulled up anchor and started the engine. He'd spent his life maneuvering in these waters and welcomed the night ahead of him since he knew he wouldn't have been able to sleep. Luc had too much thinking to do and would need the whole night to figure things out.

If Jasmine slept at all during the night, she didn't remember. All she knew was that when she awakened at seven with her pillow still sopped by tears, the engine had stopped and there was only the motion of the cruiser rocking gently back and forth.

She freshened up and caught her hair back with a clip. Once dressed in a top and shorts, she packed her few things and went up on deck to discover they were back in Nice without incident. Not that there would have been any problem with Luc at the wheel. He'd been sailing these waters all his life.

He'd already tied up the cruiser against the dock. In the distance she could see his tall physique coming back from his car, where he must have taken a load of things from the boat. More guilt consumed her because he was doing all the work. He should have wakened her to help, but he was too much of a gentleman for that.

His jet-black gaze scrutinized her from the crown of her head to the soles of her sandaled feet. He might as well have been touching her for the way it felt. "I knew you wanted to get home as soon as possible, so I packed up any provisions left to take to the villa."

"Thank you. I couldn't possibly eat right now. Is there anything else I can help take to your car? You must be exhausted after having to be awake all night."

"I'm fine and it's all done. Are you ready?"

"Yes."

He took her bag for her and steadied her arm while she stepped on to the dock. Then he let go of her and they walked to the parking area separately. Once they got in the car and were on their way, he turned to her. "Would you like to stop for coffee on the way back to Grasse?"

"I don't need anything, but thank you."

After a few miles he said, "Are you definitely leaving Sunday?"

"Yes."

"Then this will be our last time together."

"Don't get me started, Luc. I don't want to say goodbye to you, but I *have* to."

"I know. You've done a wonderful thing for Remy and the company. You've honored your grandfather's wishes. Now there's nothing left except to go home and love your family. I understand more than you think.

"After my accident, my parents stood beside me and refused to let me wallow in self-pity forever. They gave me life and were my mainstay of existence through that tumultuous period. I've tried to be a devoted son ever since.

"You're doing the honorable thing, Jasmine. I can only imagine how thrilled they'll be to know you won't be leaving again. You've got years to enjoy the life you were born into. I want you to know how much I admire you for what you've done. I'm sure your papa couldn't be happier with the way things turned out. Working with you has helped me to know him and Remy, two great men. I thank you for that."

If he didn't stop talking, she was going to scream in pain.

"That goes both ways, Luc. I don't know another man who would have done what you did to help me. Your decency and goodness is a revelation. I don't know how you thank someone for that. I only know I'm in awe of you."

"I think we're even. Since we're coming into Grasse, tell me how to reach the Fleury farm. I'd like to see it before I take you home."

Her heart pounded out of rhythm while she gave him directions. Pretty soon they were driving along the side of the violets where she'd seen Remy. Luc unexpectedly pulled over and stopped. "I'll only be a minute."

What on earth?

In fascination she watched him get out and walk over to pick a small bunch of them. When he returned to the car, he inhaled their fragrance. "These will always remind me of you." He handed them to her. "Sweet, like a spring morning." He pressed a warm kiss to her mouth, then started up the car once more.

Jasmine sat there in shock while he drove her the rest of the way to the house. He pulled up next to her Audi. "This is it. What a journey since Yeronisos. I don't know about you, but I wouldn't have missed it."

Instead of lingering, he got out and reached for the small suitcase he'd put in the back seat. After he opened the passenger door for her, she had no choice but to climb out with the flowers and her straw bag. Luc walked her to the entrance of the house.

He put it down next to her. "I detest long goodbyes. Have a safe flight home, Jasmine."

With her hands still full, he cupped her face in his hands and kissed her once more, this time hotly on the mouth.

Her legs were close to giving way by the time he got back in his car and disappeared around the bend in the gravel drive. She fell against the door, needing to hold on to the handle for support.

Luc... Luc...

On Saturday afternoon, Luc drove into the Martin ranch on the outskirts of Driggs, Idaho. The stunning view of the Teton mountain range dominated the sage-covered landscape. He found the pine-scented air warm even at the six-thousand-foot elevation. *Glorious.*

The two-story log ranch house had the authentic rustic flavor of the American West. He saw signs of various ranching equipment and several trucks parked around the side. After parking the rental car, he got out and walked up the porch to the main entrance. A dog started barking inside before Luc rang the buzzer.

He heard a woman admonishing the dog to be quiet. Soon, the door opened and he came face-to-face with a woman, fiftyish, wearing a western shirt and jeans. She was a real beauty in her own right, with a great figure, and couldn't be anyone else but Jasmine's mother.

This had to be Blanchette, the youngest daughter of Maxim and Megan Ferrier. Luc knew so much about this family it felt strange to be this close to a first descendant of the famous couple.

Blanchette had inherited her mother Megan's blond hair. But she'd bequeathed the shape of her face and features to her daughter Jasmine.

"*Bonjour*, Madame Martin," he spoke in his native tongue. "Forgive me for arriving at your doorstep without calling first, but I couldn't find your phone listed. I've flown all the way from Nice to meet you and your husband. My name is Lucien Charriere. Your daughter Jasmine and I have been doing business over the last few weeks."

"Ahh—" was the only sound she made while

her brown eyes lit up before playing over him. *"You're* Raimond Charriere's grandson who took over at the bank after his death—"

"Oui."

"According to her, you made it possible for Remy to become the new head of Ferriers. My father suffered terrible grief over that situation. Thank you for the part you played in helping Jasmine right a horrible wrong. Please. Come in. *Entrez.*"

"Merci." He followed her inside to a great room that was three stories high to let in the sun. She indicated one of the leather sofas. *"As- seyez-vous, monsieur."*

"Luc."

"Call me Blanchette. I dislike formality." She sounded so much like Jasmine just then, it stunned him. "My husband, Clark, has gone into Driggs for supplies and groceries. We're going to have a big party on Monday night to welcome Jasmine home. She'll fly into Jackson early Monday morning on the company jet. Clark should be back soon." When she sat down, the black lab lay down at her feet.

"I knew I was taking a chance. I'm sure you're wondering why I'm here, so I'll come straight to the point. I've taken time off from the bank for a vacation. There's only one way to say this. I've fallen in love with your daughter and hope she'll end up marrying me. I'm here to obtain your permission. Because your approval means everything in the world to her, it means everything to me."

She put a hand to her throat in surprise. "Have you already proposed to her?"

"No. I haven't even told her I'm in love with her. She's made it clear that her home is here in Idaho with you. When we were last together she told me we were two ships passing in the night, but I could never accept that. I realized that if I hope to get a yes out of her, then I'll have to move here.

"I love her too much to lose her, Blanchette. If she'll have me, I'm prepared to live in Idaho and earn my living here in order to be with her."

A soft cry escaped her lips. "You'd step down as CEO of the Banque Internationale du Midi and move here for her sake?"

"She told me you gave up a life in France to marry your American husband and live here with him. As you found out, when you're in love, the other things don't matter if you can't be together. I'm not different and have been considering several options of work here.

"In the meantime, for most of the day, I've been with a Realtor in Jackson who has shown me several small ranches for sale around Driggs. I'm thinking of buying one so Jasmine and I could live close to you. That's more important to her than anything else in the world. Since she's the most important thing in my life, I'll do anything because I can't live without her."

Her mother got to her feet, visibly shaken. "Does she know you've flown here?"

"No. And I don't want her to know. Not yet... We said a final goodbye a few mornings ago after coming back from a little trip along the Mediterranean to Palmaria in my cruiser. She's an amazing woman. It was a selfless act, to get Remy installed as CEO of Ferriers in order to honor your father's wishes, but naturally you already know that about your daughter."

"She's exceptional."

"I agree, and I think you and your husband are exceptional to have given her the life she's been able to live. After she's been home a few days, I'd like to come by and see her with your permission.

"But I'll wait for a call from you before I do anything in case you learn that she wouldn't be happy to see me. If she wants nothing to do with me, then I'll leave and I won't be back. Most important, I never want her to know I was here." He got up to leave.

She studied him for a long time. "Where are you staying?" He had the feeling she understood a lot he hadn't told her because she'd been through a similar experience.

"At the Teton Valley Cabins. Just ask for me at the front desk."

"Clark will be sorry he missed you."

"I'm sorry too. I'd like to meet her hero, the ultimate cowboy."

Blanchette broke into a smile so much like Jasmine's it was uncanny. "I promise to call you."

"I can't ask for more than that."

"*À la prochaine*, Luc."

Next time? Hoping there was going to be one, he left the house and took off in the rental car. There was another property he wanted to check out before dark. Tomorrow there'd be more to look at. He'd stay busy until that phone call came.

At seven on Monday morning, Jasmine's plane touched down on the tarmac in Jackson Hole, Wyoming. She walked down the steps of the Ferrier jet into the arms of her family who'd come out *en masse* to welcome her home.

She had a ton of luggage and boxes of precious mementos that Remy and his family had helped her load onto the jet before she'd left Nice. She in turn had given him her Audi for an extra car he'd need. Other Ferrier family members had gathered, even Giles, who had presented her with a bouquet of jasmine on behalf of her papa. That unexpected gift broke her down. She'd been the recipient of more gifts than one human being deserved. There'd been a lot of tears.

As the jet took off, she'd looked out on Nice, the jewel of the Mediterranean, and her life had flashed before her eyes. Luc was down there. Her beloved Luc. She knew the exact spot and felt such a stab of pain she thought she was going to pass out.

For the rest of the flight home she remained in a numbed state. Nothing seemed real as her brothers and family scrambled to pack everything in three sets of cars for the drive back to Driggs just twenty minutes away. Another beautiful August morning with the sun outlining the backside of the magnificent Tetons.

The view was so different from the flower fields she'd looked out on one last time from her bedroom balcony yesterday. Both views were spectacular.... Both represented matchless slices of life and experiences.

You're a lucky girl, Jasmine Martin. You've been given every blessing except one. Don't dwell on what can't be. Don't be greedy. You're home where you belong. It's enough. Embrace it.

Her dad opened the front door and the dog came flying. "Buck!" she cried and gave him a hug. "I've missed you too." She played with him for a minute before she insisted on a couple of boxes being opened. Jasmine had brought presents for everyone and wanted her nieces and nephews to enjoy their gifts now.

Several hours later, everyone left, but not for long. She found out her parents had planned a big party for the evening and had invited neighbors as well. Grabbing a suitcase, she walked upstairs to the same bedroom she'd had when she was a little girl. Nothing had changed.

Her dad followed her and stood in the doorway to her room. The smile on his face warmed her heart. "Hey, Sparkles. Do you have any idea how thrilled we are that this day has come?"

"I feel the same way, Dad."

"I know you do, but I see something else too."

She averted her eyes. "What do you mean?"

"Since the last time we saw you, you've changed from a girl to a mysterious woman."

A nervous laugh escaped. "There's nothing mysterious about me."

"Oh, yes, there is. You stood quietly in the doorway of the jet for a minute and I noticed it right away. I haven't had a heart-to-heart talk with you for a long time. How about it? I've got all the time in the world."

Jasmine flicked her gaze to him in consternation. "I don't know what you're getting at."

"Who's the man you left behind?"

Heat swept into her face. She'd never been able to hide anything from her father, let alone lie to him. "He's exactly that. Someone I left behind."

"Tell me about him."

"I'd rather not."

"Why? Because it's too painful to talk about?"

She took a deep breath. "Yes."

"What's he like?"

Jasmine sank down on the side of the queen-sized bed. "Grandma Megan said it best when she talked about Papa. Her words could be mine."

"What did she tell you?"

"'He's in a class by himself, Jasmine. No other man could hope to compete. It would be futile. In comparison, he makes all the other men I've ever known seem bland and unexciting. It isn't fair that one man could be so endowed. It isn't his fault. His charisma is something inherent, so are his looks and personality.'"

"Well, well. Your mom and I have wondered if this day would ever come." He sat down by her and put an arm around her shoulders. "When are we going to meet him?"

She shook her head. "You're not. It's over."

"Why?"

"Because it *has* to be," she cried. "He's the head of the Banque Internationale du Midi! He's a Frenchman whose roots go back hundreds of years. He has a big family and friends and a fabulous life. He's as married to his life as you are to ranch life."

"I see."

"To want a life with him is like this big dream that couldn't possibly come true. That's why I don't want to talk about him, not ever again. Do you mind?"

"No, sweetheart. We'll consider the subject closed." He kissed her forehead and got up from the bed. "I'll be downstairs with your mom getting things ready for the party."

"Dad? Don't misunderstand. I'm so happy to be home with you and Mom."

"You think we don't know that?" He smiled. "Go on and get settled in, then come on down and I'll fix you one of my super-duper roast beef sandwiches with your mom's homemade bread."

She ran across the room and hugged him hard. "I love you."

"Ditto."

Seven hours later, the ranch house filled up

fast with family and neighbors, old friends Jasmine hadn't seen in ages, most of them wearing cowboy boots and hats. There was no formality here. Her mom had prepared a barbecue out on the back patio with corn on the cob by the tubful and plates of her homemade rolls that disappeared by the dozens. They'd lit some torches to add to the atmosphere. Country-western music played in the background.

Jasmine dressed in jeans and a western shirt. After pulling on her well-worn cowboy boots, she brushed through her hair, having left it long, and went downstairs to help. Her sisters-in-law had prepared salads and desserts while her dad and brothers fried steaks for everyone on the two grills he'd set up. The little kids ran around having fun.

A few more guests dribbled in. Jasmine was headed for the kitchen to bring out another potato salad when she saw a few more familiar ranchers wander outside to the patio. They were all in cowboy hats and boots. But there was one she didn't recognize who stood out from the others. He had black hair and was wearing a black Stetson. One of the ranchers must have brought him along.

He was a little taller, a little more well-built. She noticed he filled out his tan fringed shirt in such a way that she couldn't possibly look anywhere else. As he started to fill his plate, she saw the play of muscle across his shoulders and back.

She moved closer, feeling the hairs stand on the back of her neck. He reminded her of Luc on the day they'd gone to see the property she'd wanted to buy. Maybe she was missing him so much that she thought she was seeing him. After the talk with her father earlier in the day, she hadn't been able to get him off her mind.

There couldn't be two Lucs in the world, could there?

Jasmine had to find out and walked over to him. "Hi! I'm Jasmine Martin. I don't think we'v—"

But she didn't get the last word out because he'd turned toward her with the plate still in his hand. The second she saw that five o'clock shadow and those black eyes, she was afraid she was hallucinating. His seductive half smile turned her entire body to jelly.

"Luc—" she whispered in a state of absolute shock.

"*Oui.*"

Her eyes grew bigger. "I—I don't believe it," she stammered. Suddenly she understood about the talk with her dad in the bedroom. Luc had already been to see her parents!

"What don't you believe? Your folks invited me to come to your welcome-home party. Naturally I wouldn't have missed it. They thought you'd probably be lonely on your first night home after being away so long." He started eating.

"Luc—" She struggled to find words. "You're really here."

"Where else would I be?"

"But when did you get here?"

"On Saturday."

"You came before *I* did?"

"That's right. I don't like goodbyes."

She began to tremble. "You—you shouldn't have come!"

"Does that mean you want me to leave right now?" He put down his plate.

"You *know* that's not what I meant."

"Then what *did* you mean?"

"Shh. Everyone's watching us." She looked around guiltily. "Come with me."

"I'm glad you said that, but it has to be some-place alone. There are a few things I need to say to you and I don't want an audience."

She bit her lip. "Follow me."

"Where are we going?"

"Upstairs."

"As long as I can get you to myself, I don't care where we go."

A deep blush crept into her face as they left the dining room. She felt him right behind her all the way up the stairs. The second he shut the door, he threw his hat across the room and reached for her.

"Luc—" she cried, but didn't make another

sound as he lowered his head and smothered her with a kiss that went on and on. They ended up on her bed.

He turned her on her back so he could look down at her. "I swear you're the most bewitching woman I ever met in my life. I love you more than life, Jasmine. You have to marry me, the sooner the better. I'm asking you right here and now."

"But—"

"No buts, *mon tresor*. Just so you know, we'll be living here from now on. I've been looking at ranches. There's one four miles down the road from here that would be perfect for us. My family will fly over for the wedding. We'll do what your parents did and fly back and forth to visit family. It can work."

"How can you say that when your life is in France?"

"Not anymore. You and I are not ships passing in the night. We're madly in love and we'll never be happy if we don't live together forever starting this instant. Say you'll marry me,

Jasmine. Without you, life will never mean the same to me again."

"I feel the same way," she exclaimed. "I love you beyond reason. Yes I'll marry you." She threw her arms around his neck and kissed his eyes. "Yes." She kissed his nose. "Yes." She kissed his mouth, heedless of everything except her love for this incredible man. "I love you with all my heart and soul, darling. There's not another man alive like you. I've already found out that to be without you is a living death."

In another instant his total demeanor changed.

"Dieu merci," he whispered against her throat. She felt his body tremble against hers. *"Je t'aime, mon amour."* His voice had grown husky. *"Je t'adore."*

CHAPTER NINE

December 24

"COME TO BED, JASMINE."

"I will. I just have to finish wrapping this Christmas present for your mother." The French wedding reception to celebrate their August marriage had been held earlier in the evening at Luc's parents' villa in Cagnes-sur-Mer. Now they had to get ready for Christmas Day.

"I thought everything was done."

"It is, but this little gift is special and wasn't ready until I dropped by the perfumery yesterday. I had to find the right packaging for it. Since you said periwinkle is her favorite color, I hunted for the right paper. I'll be through here in a minute."

He walked over to the dressing table where she was sitting and put his hands on her shoulders. By now, her body was so sensitive to his touch, she trembled if he even came near her. The mirror reflected the two of them. Her heart thudded heavily as she anticipated going to bed with him tonight.

Every night since the wedding had been like their wedding night. Luc was an insatiable lover who took her to the heights and taught her the meaning of selfless loving.

"You've been very secretive about this gift."

"That's because your mother is a very special person. I want to honor her because she gave birth to the most wonderful man in existence. I love your parents."

He kissed the curve of her neck. "They love you. Won't you give me a hint what it is?"

She put the package down and turned in his arms. "If you really want to know, I developed a perfume ages ago and was waiting for the right person to give it to. After realizing how much your mother loves roses, I knew it would be the perfect present for her."

His black eyes traveled over every feature. "Are you talking Rose de Mai?"

"Yes." She brushed her lips against his. "You remember!"

"They were growing off the terrace at La Tourette. The scent was clear and sweet."

"Just like your mother, darling. But what you loved was the light note of honey."

"Which only you could detect."

"That's why it's so sweet. I called Remy several months ago and asked him to take Fabrice some flowers from the garden with instructions to make up a small fresh batch of my rose recipe and have it ready by the time we flew over."

"Who's Fabrice?"

"One of the chemists."

"Do I want to know about him?"

She smiled. "No, you fool."

"Maman won't believe it when you give her a bottle of her own perfume made by the greatest nose since the death of your papa. That's an honor she'll never forget."

"I certainly wasn't the greatest that night at

La Tourette after you brought me home from dinner."

"That's all behind us, *mignonne*." He turned off the lights before picking her up in his arms. When they reached the bed, he followed her down. "Do you miss the lab?"

"No," she answered honestly. "Do you miss walking into the bank every day?"

"You know I don't. Thanks to the miracle of technology I can consult from our den in Driggs, and have time to grow an alfalfa crop in the backyard. I've got to learn all I can. When our children come along, I want to be able to measure up to your father."

She held his handsome face between her hands. "You don't need to measure up to anyone. You're magnificent just the way you are. I'm so crazy about you. Love me tonight, darling. I want your baby."

With those words Luc made love to her with abandon. At the height of their passion, he kissed her almost savagely, but she welcomed it. She wanted to trap him in her arms and never let him go. He was so strong and so incredibly gorgeous she could look at him and love him all night.

Toward morning, he let out a long deep sigh and tangled his legs with hers. "Jasmine," he murmured against her lips.

"What is it?"

"I have a little Christmas present for you right now. I've memorized something I want you to hear."

She blinked and sat up so she could look at him. "You have me intrigued. What is it?"

He rubbed his hand over her hip possessively. "Your papa was the poet. I've taken license with his words. 'Jasmine is the flower for nostalgia. Like the flower that grows in doorways and winds over arches, she links me to the intimacy of our love nest. Her cheeks bloom as the days become hotter, and she releases her scent at the hour when tables are set in the garden, or in narrow lanes, or in the dark of night in my arms. She reminds me of the melancholy of dusk if she's not with me. Her presence brings out the conviviality of summer evenings when I'm with her. Her fragrance permeates the air, making it a background for the love I feel for her.'"

"Oh, Luc." She started sobbing, so deeply touched she started making love to him.

The sun was well up in the sky before she let him go.

"Do you want to know a secret on this joyous Christmas morning?"

They were both worn out. *"Bien sûr,"* he murmured, close to being too exhausted to talk.

"I love scents…but there's no flower on earth that can compete with my favorite scent."

At that remark his lids flickered open. "What's sweeter than a flower?"

"I've labeled it 'The Scent of Her Man.'"

"Does that mean you developed a cologne for men a long time ago? Something synthetic?"

"No, darling. It can't be created or manufactured." She pressed her mouth to his. "It's the scent of *you*. There's no other scent like it on earth because there will never be another Lucien Charriere. You're my heart's blood, but I think you already know that by now.

"In fact, I think you sensed it before you ever left Yeronisos island. If only you knew how much I'd wished you'd been lying in wait for me *after* I came back down. You can't imagine my disappointment."

"Now she tells me," he cried and proceeded to plunder her mouth over and over again.

* * * * *

MILLS & BOON®
Large Print – May 2015

THE SECRET HIS MISTRESS CARRIED
Lynne Graham

NINE MONTHS TO REDEEM HIM
Jennie Lucas

FONSECA'S FURY
Abby Green

THE RUSSIAN'S ULTIMATUM
Michelle Smart

TO SIN WITH THE TYCOON
Cathy Williams

THE LAST HEIR OF MONTERRATO
Andie Brock

INHERITED BY HER ENEMY
Sara Craven

TAMING THE FRENCH TYCOON
Rebecca Winters

HIS VERY CONVENIENT BRIDE
Sophie Pembroke

THE HEIR'S UNEXPECTED RETURN
Jackie Braun

THE PRINCE SHE NEVER FORGOT
Scarlet Wilson

MILLS & BOON®
Large Print – June 2015

THE REDEMPTION OF DARIUS STERNE
Carole Mortimer

THE SULTAN'S HAREM BRIDE
Annie West

PLAYING BY THE GREEK'S RULES
Sarah Morgan

INNOCENT IN HIS DIAMONDS
Maya Blake

TO WEAR HIS RING AGAIN
Chantelle Shaw

THE MAN TO BE RECKONED WITH
Tara Pammi

CLAIMED BY THE SHEIKH
Rachael Thomas

HER BROODING ITALIAN BOSS
Susan Meier

THE HEIRESS'S SECRET BABY
Jessica Gilmore

A PREGNANCY, A PARTY & A PROPOSAL
Teresa Carpenter

BEST FRIEND TO WIFE AND MOTHER?
Caroline Anderson